The Next Best Man

Other Novels by Bob Erlich

No Vacancy

The Next Best Man

Bob Erlich

6

ISBN 096697493X
EAN-13 9780966974935

Acknowledgements

I wish to thank my former colleagues in government service for the initial inspiration to attempt the challenge of writing this book. However brief and infrequent my service was, it left an indelible impression on me and for that I am grateful.

To Cesare, Fred, and Jerry, for your inspiration, guidance, and a lifetime of memories.

Prologue

There is no way to adequately describe a mountainous jungle or rainforest if you've never spent time in one. I don't mean the eco-tourist, let's see the trees and monkeys type of trip, where you arrive back in your four-star eco-lodge for the evening in time to take a hot shower and catch Happy Hour at the Tiki bar. The jungle I know, the one I've known over and over again for so many years is the one that covers you like a shroud. It's the one that sucks the energy from you like a lamp does from a wall socket. My jungle is steamy and draining. It stinks of wet, rotting vegetation, devours as much light as a solar eclipse, closes in around you and saps the smug certainty and self confidence from you as surely as true loneliness can.

My jungle can also be welcoming and wonderful, a kaleidoscope of colors and sounds, almost cacophonous. Its paths and rivers can reveal unimagined natural beauty and tranquility of a different sort, a sense of calm and well-being you can't get anywhere else.

So you want to see the real thing, have the unadulterated experience? Walk the path less traveled? Well, good for you. Just remember, blazing trail in the jungle is terribly hard, a challenge to your body and spirit with every step, every steep climb. Its dangers, natural and man-made are often unseen and can frequently be fatal if underestimated or ignored. The jungle can break even the strongest person in less than a week, reduce you to a lethargic drone with no fight or will to continue. But if you can find a way to adapt, bend with the oppressive force that constantly pushes against you, the reward can be all you ever dreamed of and more. It's just there, over the next hill, around the next river bend. There lies discovery, beauty, and truth, the unwrapping of a hundred Christmas gifts all at once. And you may find out more about who you are than you may wish to know.

Very few among us can truly say they've seen virgin rainforest and triple canopy jungle, been in that voluminous gut of nature. The quest for discovery shapes you, makes you see things differently forever afterwards. Just look at what happened to Percy Fawcett, or to Hiram Bingham to a lesser (and less tragic) degree. Mind you, your new view of the world will not always be for the best, but it will different without question. So you might read what follows and come away with some impression of what the experience can be like or you might not. It's not my fault if you don't, since it's almost impossible to string together enough of the right words to describe the experience of being one of the first to explore new places. But if you decide that the best way to understand all of this is to go for it and try it yourself, then I wish you all the best. Just don't ask me to come along.

Chapter 1

"So Mr. Rose, let's begin again, and this time try ta' remember everythin' that happened." The sharply dressed agent had repeated his request one time too many for Eli's tastes, and he finally, stupidly lost his temper.

"Look - How many times do I have to cover the same bullshit with you? I told you everything I knew hours ago. This is the third goddamn time already. What's your fucking problem?"

The razor-sharp Station Chief stared at Eli coldly, like he was looking at some annoying insect on the far wall of his office. "*You*, Mr. Rose, ah ma' fuckin' problem. Or rather, *you* ah a huge thorn in the ass a the United States government and a major pain in ma' ass. Do ya' have any idea just how much trouble ya' in here, boy? How much trouble *ahm* in?"

"Up yours," Eli replied angrily. "I've been poked and prodded and interrogated by the PLA and you people for the past month and I'm sick of it. Either give me back to the Reds or let me go."

The Station Chief liked to handle these types of situations personally. Routine stuff was meant for the rookies he'd been forced to train. There'd been a constant stream of them since he'd inherited the job from his predecessor, the young punk with the powerful Congressman uncle to pull strings for him. He didn't have the same advantages coming up when he was a young field agent and every time he remembered that it pissed him off. He'd had to grind it out, one shithole post at a time. It had been thirty years; thirty years of crap spent working his way up to be a Senior Chief of Station. What a life! The Congo, Bogotá, Manila. He'd seen a lot of messed up stuff in his time. But in this post it was mostly the simple shit, like maritime infractions, lost tourists, and smugglers.

However, this was a first. He'd never had a major military incident involving a US citizen before now. But finally, there it was on his watch. He was angry and embarrassed about it but also thrilled that he finally had something to deal with that was a better use of his skills then all that routine crap. As much of a problem as this was, he really *loved* that something had finally happened that he could brag about to his buddies at Langley.

"Start at the start, Rose," he said slowly. "All the way from the beginnin', and don't leave anythin' out."

Eli put his head in his hands and sighed. He realized he had no choice and was condemned by his actions to tell the story again. It was like a version of Purgatory, where you are stuck between salvation and damnation. "Ok, once again from the start, I was sitting in the bar when................"

§

"Don't gimme' that crap, ya' drunken bastard! Ante up or get outta' duh damn game." The fat guy glared at Eli over his cards, glistening with sweat in the still night air like he'd just run a marathon. The loud, 70's-style Dior shirt he wore stuck to his chest like a second skin. Eli guessed that 1989 hadn't yet arrived where he lived.

"Come on Rose, play 'em or lay 'em down!"

"Yeah, Ok," Eli groaned. His head hurt from the rum and the smoke from those Cuban *Cohiba's* made his stomach turn. All the money Eli had left in the world was shoved into that little pile in the center of the table. Everything was riding on that beautiful king-high full house. "There," said Eli, thrusting forward his last 100 *colones*. "That's all I've got. What do you have?"

The fat guy sneered at Eli and pulled a huge wad of cash from his sweat-stained pocket. He wiped his wet forehead on the sleeve of the expensive shirt and looked over at his friend, who was occupied with one of the local whores. "Hey, Art, whadda' ya' think I should do here?"

Art, who was no small man in his own right, left the two hookers at the bar and waddled over to the table. He stared at the five cards in his friend's hand and said coldly, "Bust his balls."

"Ok, Rose. Read 'em and weep." The fat slob tossed the cards down on the table recklessly, like someone who was convinced he'd lost, but Eli guessed from his casual manner that the opposite was true. He folded his cards into the palm of his hand and poured another glass of rum.

The fat guy laughed deeply and shook so hard that the sweat beads on his face flew out onto the floor like raindrops. "I told ya' deese locals was easy pickin's," he bellowed to Art. "Thanks for duh chump change, Rose," he added, stuffing the money into the pockets of his baggy shorts. "It was a pleasure meetin' ya'." The giant toad got up and ushered his horny friend towards the door and said, "What I tell ya' Art? Costa Rica is a fuckin' paradise for Americans. Did I lie, or what?" They both laughed as they burst out into the calm night, heading back to their skiff for the short ride to their behemoth of a boat in the bay.

Eli swallowed the rest of the rum and poured another, recklessly spilling some onto the floor. Miguel shuffled slowly over to the table and calmly removed the old glasses and spent cigar butts so that Eli could lay his tired head down for a short nap. Dizzy and confused from another night of excess, he managed to close his eyes and slip away into sleep. Maybe the alcohol would finally catch up with him. Maybe this was how the end would come, not in some ear-splitting firefight but from "natural causes" in a stinking, bug-infested bar in the tropics. He no longer cared what happened. Sleep was the only escape.

"Hey, what the hell? Wha', what is it? What do you want?" Eli's head was pounding like a bass drum and his vision was blurred. Someone was shaking him and saying something in Spanish. "Ok, Ok, I'm up already." Eli propped his unshaven chin up on one hand and stared bleary-eyed at his tormentor.

"*Señor* Eli, you are Ok?" said the boy.

"*Si, Si*. What do you want, Omar?"

"*Mi mamá* say no forget the fish you promise for tonight." The boy stood there expectantly, wide-eyed and smiling like he knew Eli well.

"Yeah, yeah, Ok. I'll remember." Eli tried to stretch out but was stiff and sore from spending the night on the hard bench. He felt like he'd done 70 years of hard labor at some penitentiary. As Eli's head cleared he realized he must have been dreaming about the Cuba escapade again, it's vivid landscape ever more real as he passed his life away in exile. No Eva, no Jasper, no Morgan. No longer was he the young protégé of Vicente Amarón. Eli's new reality quickly slipped back to him, just like it always had before.

"Miguel," waved Eli, "a beer, *pronto!*" He uncapped another icy bottle of Imperial, stumbled off his bar stool and fell into the booth next to the window. Eli swore on his life never to drink so heavily again, a familiar refrain to Miguel and the others, and gulped the cold brew. What a night it had been. He had played cards with the two stupid *gringo* tourists and drank until dawn, reminiscing about Miami and the old days. It really affected Eli, but the present was very different, *very different,* and his luck hadn't changed one bit. He'd been a veritable castaway since he'd told Morgan he was through with The Agency and now his money and his luck were quickly disappearing into the crystal blue Pacific.

Eli stared out across the black sand beach of Playa Coco at the children playing in the gentle surf. Fluffy white clouds hung low over the sunny bay, and contrasted sharply with his oppressive mood. *Restaurante Pappagallo* was his salvation and damnation, all in one, his oasis, his way station on the rocky road to nowhere. A cool breeze blew in the open window, refreshing and awakening Eli's will to live just for one more day.

The ceiling fans turned lazily and Eli watched Miguel wipe down the long mahogany bar with a damp, dirty rag. Eli stared disparagingly at the rusting wood and steel barrels Miguel passed off as bar stools, and remembered how dangerous they faithfully proved to be for all the drunken sots like him. The nautical trappings of brass propellers, ships wheels, and compasses masked the fact that Miguel actually hated the water. He only owned the place through an act of sheer providence anyway, having won it from the previous Yankee owner with a lowly pair of two's in a drunken poker game.

When Eli owned the place, *Restaurante Pappagallo* had been the hottest spot on the Pacific coast of Costa Rica, a stomping ground for the rich and famous and infamous alike. In the future it would boom again after the dawn of eco-tourism, but the current cruel reality for Eli was that the place had given way to time and was crumbling slowly into the black Playa Coco sands. Entropy reigned supreme and enveloped the place, and Eli thought that one day soon it would wash out to sea with the outgoing tide, fading into the past of the innocuous little village he had come to call home.

For the moment, however, Eli loved *Pappagallo* like he had once loved Miami. It represented the last recollection, the last vestige of his former life that he could still reach out and touch every morning. The restaurant was as rough and frayed at the edges as Eli; worn, yet comfortable like an old sneaker. In its present form, *Pappagallo* served as a gathering place for the misguided and dangerous. Tourists seeking the flavor of Costa Rica wandered in from time to time, but mostly there were the *narcotraficantes* and people like Eli who drifted in, seeking safe harbor and a quiet refuge from the storm often referred to as the "real world." He stared at the dripping bottle of lager, watching the condensation form and slip off its sides like a heavy dew. Eli's thoughts turned to little Omar, and his mother Violeta, and the fish he had promised to bring them for dinner, so he drank down the last few drops of the cold liquid and tossed the bottle to Miguel. "Let's go, Omar. See you soon Miguel," Eli said, and Miguel waved as he trudged out onto the dirt road.

The dreams had grown worse by the week, and their recent reprise had really unsettled Eli. These episodes always caused him to reflect on his circumstances, to wonder why he was in Costa Rica wasting his life away. He needed a shave; a new shirt and a decent pair of pants wouldn't have hurt, either. Unfortunately, those things cost money that was in short supply, and he wasn't about to go back to the work he despised so much for them. Upon reflection, Eli decided his life wasn't really so bad after all.

He bought a fish on credit from the old fisherman, Patricio, who lived down the hill and slogged up the dusty road to Violeta's house in the palms, his *current* temporary lodging. The little cottage was strategically located overlooking Playa Coco and in the past provided a good vantage point from which to view the incoming boat traffic in the bay. Eli cast a quick look over his shoulder at "The Club" at Hotel El Ocotal, the last vestige of late 20th century western money for a hundred miles, and the only place in the area that the rare tourists and water-logged sailors could still find a hot shower and satellite television. Hotel El Ocotal was the upscale modern replacement for the old Hotel Corazón, with all the trappings of the modern world but none of the character of the old place.

Eli walked down the path to Violeta's place, and admired for the first time in months the colorful wild hibiscus and orchids she nurtured by the front door. The last time he had noticed them was the night the Corazón had burned down, supposedly the result of a fit thrown by a drunken Colombian drug dealer pissed at having been denied a room. The glow from the fire was almost as spectacular as the sunsets they watched every evening from Violeta's back porch. Eli remembered the last time he'd stayed at the place, that last day with Eva. It seemed now that it all happened in a dream, or in someone else's life.

"Violeta? Violeta? Where are you my love?" Eli tossed the fish into the kitchen sink and listened for her reply. The black-haired beauty was in the garden picking bananas and didn't hear him arrive, so she continued humming cheerily to herself. Her long black hair flowed around her shoulders like a smooth-flowing stream, and Eli wondered how he could have been so fortunate to find her. "Violeta, my love – how are you?"

"Eli!" She smiled and hugged him around the neck. "I am very fine...and how you are?"

"How *are* you?" he repeated, correcting her gently. Eli smiled and nodded his approval of her attempt at learning English. He pulled her close as she moved towards the house and kissed her long and hard on the lips. She dropped her vegetable basket on the dirt but didn't seem to notice.

"You see," she said in mock anger, "the things fall to the floor." She stooped to pick them up and Eli patted her perfect round rear softly.

"You see, I have big fish for you."

"*Si*," she grinned broadly, staring at his zipper, "Eli has big fish. We see after the dinner, no?"

"Ok," he chuckled. She began to sort and wash the vegetables and fruits, humming to herself like before, so Eli strolled out onto the fragile wooden porch to fire up the grill. "*Omar,* come here," Eli called, and the boy ran to him, panting like a playful puppy. "Go find some wood for the fire," he instructed, "but make it good wood. You know...."

"*Si, Señor* Eli, I know," he gasped, and ran off down the hill in a cloud of dust. Eli stirred and sifted the ashes in the old Zayers-brand bar-b-que and stared at the random arrangement as if they were tea leaves in some fortune teller's cup. Life on Playa Coco was certainly simple, and sweet in its own way. Violeta and Omar made a perfect, if unofficial family and the stress of a "modern" lifestyle was always kept at arm's length in the village. But Eli was still concerned about the dreams-cum-nightmares, which he knew were a sign of troubled waters ahead. One thing at a time - first, it would be a fish on the grill. Maybe later he would deal with the demons of his past.

The fire had burnt low and dull and the sun had plunged into the western ocean by the time they finished the savory meal. Violeta and Eli relaxed on the porch swing arm-in-arm while Omar chased moths with a flashlight Eli had won in a poker game. They sat silently for a while, watching the sky turn colors in the cool April night breeze. Omar trotted up as the light faded and asked if he could go to the *farmacia* down the road and watch his favorite show on the television. "*Si,*" said Violeta with a sigh as he ran out to the road. "You have three hours and no more."

"*Si, mami!*" He shot off down the road and was

gone in a second. "What a boy!" she laughed, and the couple smiled as the dust cloud drifted back to its source. Eli was still unsettled by the unaccustomed introspection he'd subjected himself to earlier, and the dark-eyed lady could sense it easily. "Eli, you are worry?"

"It's nothing," he lied, hugging her tightly. "Don't worry about me. Everything is Ok. You understand?"

"No!" she huffed, he eyes ablaze. "I know you have *problema*. Tell me, my love"

"Really," Eli insisted, "it's nothing. No big deal. Don't worry, Ok? Don't worry." She pulled away from him and turned so she could face him, nose to nose. She slid down Eli's chest like a heavy woolen blanket until she reached his zipper.

"I will fix," she sighed. Her hair smelled sweet like banana flowers and Eli hugged her tightly, immersed in Violeta's soft, supple body. She led Eli by the hand to the bed and they collapsed together in the throes of passion. Some clothes were removed, the rest regarded as unimportant as the two lovers worked each other to the edge of ecstasy. Violeta's brown skin looked flawless in the poorly illuminated room; the image of her nude body in the rich twilight burned into his brain. For a fleeting moment Eli thought of the stories he'd heard about men dying while in the midst of love making, understanding how that was possible. Violeta thrust herself at him until neither one could endure it any longer. One final, rhythmic push brought them both to their release, and they relaxed, soaked with sweat and exhausted. They kissed quietly in the shadows and she whispered, "Is better?"

"*Si*, my love, is better now," he lied. "Everything is Ok."

Chapter 2

Eli thought that perhaps Violeta's remedy had cured him of the nightmares as several days had passed without a recurrence. He resolved to make a clean start of the new week, and had made an appointment to see an American travel agent he knew who had offered him a job as a guide for the tours she ran. Her well-heeled clients could provide a more secure source of income to Eli than the infrequent and unpredictable poker games at *Restaurante Pappagallo*. Such serious negotiations required some stout preparations, however, and Eli soon found himself perched atop one of Miguel's barrel-style bar stools for a quick glass of rum and soda.

"*Miguel,* what's new?" said Eli, growing fond of the rickety stool. "*El regular, amigo.*"

"*Si, Señor.*" Miguel always kept the two liquids separate for him, knowing how much Eli hated adulterating the taste of good rum.

The sun shone brilliantly on the sand and Eli felt that the future would soon be as clear as the cloudless blue sky. "What a beautiful day," he exclaimed. Miguel nodded and smiled, but continued to wipe down the bar. Eli sipped his drink and stared out at the calm blue water, and said out loud, "Another beautiful damn day in paradise."

"What?" Miguel picked his head up from his labors for a moment, concerned that Eli might have wanted something.

"Nothing, er, *nada, amigo.*" Just as his focus had drifted back off to the bay, it was quickly broken by a soft, English-speaking voice. "Mr. Rose? Mr. Eli Rose?" Eli swiveled around on the stool, expecting to see that his travel agent friend had arrived early, but was greatly surprised to find someone else standing in front of him. "He's not here, but I'd be happy to leave a message for him," said Eli dryly, hoping the beautiful stranger would go away.

The girl instantly pulled an old black and white Polaroid out of her shoulder bag, examined it for a moment, and then said, "Please, Mr. Rose, I must speak with you."

"Look, Miss, I don't know who you think I am, but whatever your problem is, I can't help you solve it. Now please go away. I've got an important business meeting in a few minutes, and you're scaring the locals."

"Elijah Ryan Rose. Born Miami Beach, Florida. Father, Samuel, deceased; mother, Ann, deceased. Ten years as a "consultant" for the US government with some side work cleaning up "messes" for some of the richest and most powerful people in Miami. Your US office was in Coral Gables on Alhambra Drive until 1984. You've been in self-imposed exile here ever since. Should I go on?"

"That's alright. I get the picture," Eli growled. He knew that "bio" well enough – it sounded strangely familiar and hearing it recited it that way was very unwelcome. "Congratulations, you found me. Now what the hell do you want from me?"

"My, my," she purred. "You are a testy sort before noon, aren't you? But then, I'd heard that." Her lilting English accent calmed him somewhat, but Eli still wanted her to disappear.

"*Miguel* - another drink!" Eli sat back and stared into the girl's bright blue eyes. "What do you want to drink?"

"No thanks, nothing for me" she said curtly. "Perhaps we should sit in that booth over there where we can speak somewhat more privately?"

Eli waved off Miguel and dismounted the well-worn stool. He slid into the booth opposite her, so he could study her unusually impressive features more closely. "You're Hong Kong Chinese," he said slowly, eyeing her shapely form with uninhibited interest. "Probably English father, Chinese mother - Hong Kong side, right?"

"That was too easy, Mr. Rose, but not a bad effort nonetheless." She smiled broadly. "Do you always stare so rudely at prospective clients?"

"Only when they look like you."

"You are direct," she said, flicking her long black

hair over her shoulders. "And a flatterer." She leaned forward and whispered, "Right then. What I'm going to tell you must be held in the strictest confidence. You must promise not to utter a word of this to anyone, under any circumstances."

"Cross my heart," said Eli, making the motion in exaggerated style. He was captivated and distracted by her full, perfect lips and exotic air. She smelled like jasmine in full flower, the kind of smell that overpowers you and fills your head with carnal thoughts. Eli decided that the travel agent business could wait a little longer.

"My name is Mai Lee Jones. I'm here at the request of my uncle, Cheung Lido, to ask your help in retrieving a most cherished family heirloom that was recently stolen. The people that stole it have been trying to sell it on the black market in Hong Kong, but our sources say that the artifact may soon be removed from the market for private sale. We, Uncle and I, believe that if this happens, we will never be able to track the item, and it would be lost forever."

"A fair assumption. But why don't you just involve the local police?"

"Because, Mr. Rose, we believe a high police official may have been involved in the theft. We don't know who to trust in Hong Kong."

"Which is why you're going outside to find talent. Ok, tell me more."

"This family heirloom is not just a Ming vase or some other ridiculous memento, as I'm sure you've surmised by now. It is a two foot tall carving of the philosopher Confucius from the Han Dynasty period, made from a solid piece of rare Burmese jade. As you can imagine, any artifact over 1700 years old would be valuable, but this particular one is worth a very large amount of money."

"How large?" Eli asked, more curious by the minute.

"More than three million U.S. dollars at the last estimate. We think that the right buyer might pay two or three times that price." She sighed for a moment, and then continued, "A great deal of my family's wealth is tied up in similar things, though this one item represents the single greatest block. We had planned to use the proceeds from its sale to finance our new business venture in Canada. We must be ready for the hand-over when it comes."

"Makes sense," said Eli sharply, sipping deeply from his glass. "So why come all the way to east nowhere to find *me*? You're obviously serious or you wouldn't have tracked me all the way here. You're also able to afford the best in the world, so why drag up a tired old has-been?"

"Why a tired old has-been like you?" she repeated, amused by his question. "Ah, perhaps that is a good question indeed, considering what I've found. You came highly recommended to Uncle from a mutual acquaintance, a fellow by the name of Vicente Amarón."

Eli coughed up his last gulp of rum and sighed coldly.

"Yes, I know the name, and I'll ask you not to use it in my presence again." He sat back in the booth and folded his arms across his chest, now impatient and irritated by the specter of his old mentor. "Ok, so what else have you got?"

"That's basically it," she replied. "We need to leave for the airport today so we can catch the first plane out of the country."

"Whoa, not so fast. Leaving immediately is out of the question. Besides, there's the little matter of the fee? Haven't heard about that yet."

"Yes, of course. Your usual fee, prorated for inflation since your last paying job in 1984." She pulled a huge wad of US greenbacks from her bag and shoved them at Eli. "I believe this will serve as an adequate advance on the rest."

She handed him the bills as if they were a load of rotten apples, and Eli quickly enveloped them with both arms in an attempt to hide the treasure from curious eyes. He slowly began to count the bills but was interrupted by the girl. Don't bother," she sniffed, indignantly. "Ten thousand dollars. Is it enough?"

"Well," he choked, "for now, maybe. We'll talk about the rest later." Eli quickly stuffed the fist-sized roll in his pocket and stood up, motioning for her to follow. "You're covering expenses, right?" She smiled and nodded in the affirmative. "And you're no doubt staying at the Ocotal, right?"

"Yes."

"Listen, I've got a few things to attend to. I'll swing by and get you at about one o'clock. We should still be able to get into San José in plenty of time to catch tomorrow's flight to San Francisco."

"That's fine," she said as they slipped out of the restaurant. Eli waved good-bye to Miguel, and the two headed up the hill past the palm-shaded huts of Eli's neighbors. He was unsure about all this. It was moving too fast and he'd just sworn to himself that he would never to go back to that line of work. But the chance to start over, especially with that size stake was irresistible. Just one last job. One last job and he'd stop for good.

The dust rose in frantic little swirls at their feet as the ocean breeze picked up. The underbrush rustled loudly and leaves fluttered like hummingbird wings, making the path to the Ocotal seem unusually busy and alive. "So, Mr. Rose, would you care to tell me why I had to come all the way to "east nowhere" to find you?"

Eli smiled and shook his head slowly, with no intention of quenching her curiosity. "Some other time." As they approached the hotel road, Eli was distracted by an abnormally-shaped shadow plastered behind some nearby bushes. He hadn't remembered ever seeing a large growth of foliage there, and his hair suddenly bristled a familiar "you're being watched" warning. Wheeling around slightly to his right, Eli glanced back just in time to see a long-handled machete slicing toward his head. He slipped deftly under its sweep and grabbed the arm that wielded the weapon, twisting it violently to the ground. Mai Lee shrieked and jumped back, stunned, as her protector wrestled the blade from the prone attacker. Eli jerked the guy's hand up and jammed his right heel into his elbow, snapping the thug's arm at the joint. The guy screamed in pain as the bone and cartilage popped, rolling in the dust as Eli snatched the machete from the ground. Turning to face Mai Lee, Eli had just enough time to shout "Move!" as another thug swung at him from the underbrush. Eli jabbed the point of the blade up to meet his attacker's, stopping the guy's momentum only inches from his own head.

"Son of a bitch!" yelled Eli, and pivoted around to parry the next jab. The two combatants squared off like rabid dogs, threatening each other with abortive lunges and feints, looking for some obvious weakness. "Hey, asshole," said Eli. "Look at your friend," knowing he'd get the meaning quickly. The other guy was still moaning loudly in the dirt with his horribly bent arm, and Eli's new challenger shot a furtive glance in his comrade's direction. The guy stared back at Eli, licking his lips nervously, and Eli just smiled. That provoked the guy to jump at him wildly. Eli slipped to his left and swung the machete back across his chest, catching the guy low on the left side. The assassin winced in pain and groaned as he turned back, lurching violently and uncontrollably. Eli parried his wounded attacker's thrust again, but this time stepped into the guy's lunge with the machete pointed at the assassin's middle. The long blade made a sickening sound as it punctured his stomach and sliced out through his ribcage. Eli turned quickly and twisted the long blade, yanking it from his innards in one motion. He stepped back as his stunned attacker dropped to his knees, his mouth gaping. Eli swept the machete past his face like a samurai and jammed it into the ground beside him. The guy twitched suddenly and collapsed in a heap, his wide eyes reflecting the disbelief of his own death. "Quick - get back to the hotel," shouted Eli. "Grab your stuff and be ready to get out when I come back."

The girl nodded, her hand covering her mouth in shock, and ran up the hill to the hotel. *Christ*, thought Eli. *Three years of virtual isolation and near deadly boredom* and his life had once again been turned upside down in an instant. His mind raced and panic flooded over him. He felt just like he did outside Managua, the night that everything went wrong and the Sandinistas caught him. There it was again, that feeling from all the nightmares, only now it was real – the palpable raw taste of fear.

Eli's heart pounded like a steel drum but he slowed his breathing, trying not to hyperventilate. He ran down the path to Violeta's place and changed clothes in a mad rush. No one was there, so Eli scribbled a note explaining as best he could that he would be away for a while on business, and not to worry, for he'd be back soon. He took one last look at their wonderful little place by the bay and ran out, ripping back up the road to the hotel. Mai Lee had her car out in front and was waiting with the engine running when Eli arrived. "Damn, girl!" he said, exasperated. "Why'd you have to rent a piece of shit Tercel? It'll take us forever to get to San José in this thing."

"Next time I run away from some killers, I'll be certain to pick something more suitable," she snapped. Eli slammed the car into first gear and spun out of the driveway in a cloud of dust and gravel. He slid the little car recklessly along the dirt roads until they joined the main all-weather highway to San José. Eli already knew that the two assassins that had jumped them at the Ocotal weren't after him. He knew everyone in the little village and these guys weren't locals. The only question that was important to Eli was whether or not he could manage to get the girl out of the country in one piece. It would be no small task, considering the fact that whoever wanted her already knew her by sight.

Eli pushed the little car hard all the way down Highway 1, trying to gain as much time as possible on their perceived enemies. There were a thousand places along the way where they could be ambushed, so he made an effort not to get boxed in by the characteristically dense traffic near San José. The couple sat silently for over an hour, with only the roar of the wind through the windows as a background for their thoughts. Eli believed she was probably thinking the same thing that he was - how to get out of the situation as fast as possible - though neither of them expressed even slight recognition of the thought to the other. The truth seemed far away at that point, so Eli decided he had nothing to lose by continuing to search for it in the car. "Miss Jones, may I ask you something?"

She looked a bit surprised for an instant, but replied, "Please call me Mai Lee. What is it that you wish to know?"

"I'm curious about your background. You're obviously well educated – Cambridge, right? And as you have said, you're fairly well-off, too. What keeps you in Hong Kong with the hand-over imminent? Why haven't you made your way in England or America or Canada by now?"

She smiled introspectively for a second and said, "There is still time for that, Mr. Rose. Right now Hong Kong is my home. Why should I leave my home? Hong Kong has everything I could ever want - much more than most places. It's true that the Communists will likely change everything, but even that is uncertain. Why would they kill the goose that laid the golden egg? If they just leave it alone Hong Kong will reward them a thousand times over." The Asian beauty paused for a moment and smiled again. "By the way, that was a very good guess"

Eli flashed a confident grin. "I used to know a guy who attended university at Cambridge," he answered, anticipating her question. "You both have similar affectations and vocal rhythms, distinctive kinds of things to a crude Yank like me." That reminded Eli of a distant memory he'd almost let slip away, but he quickly refocused on his current companion. "Call me Eli."

She laughed aloud and smiled broadly, a beautiful smile and the first time she'd appeared relaxed since they'd met. "Yes, Eli, I suppose my mannerisms are a bit distinct. Do you always have such convoluted discussions with your employers?"

"Not usually. Only with friends."

Her eyes crinkled when she smiled, brightening her face like the warm afternoon sun of Playa Coco. Eli was taken with her charm and beauty, though he desperately needed to catch at least some minor morsel of the truth before he could relax and trust her. "What kind of work do you do in Hong Kong?"

"We are in the import/export business; I manage the books. Business administration degree, class of '81."

What a familiar business that was! "So, what kinds of things do you import and export? That sounds very complicated."

"Not really," she smiled. "We deal in modern Chinese arts and crafts, a business nearly as old as China itself. There is a fairly high demand for Chinese pottery and art in Western Europe and Canada at the moment, believe it or not. It's been a profitable enterprise for us, especially over the past three years. Our import business has centered on food items, mostly beef from Canada."

"Very interesting," feigned Eli. He knew the business as well as anyone, having done it in his younger, more innocent days. "So I'm sure you have problems with customs agents. I mean, they must give you a hard time on occasion, right?"

The girl glanced at the road for a moment. "Eli, my

credentials are available if you wish to know. I can satisfy any questions you have about the authenticity of our business interests as soon as we get to Hong Kong. You needn't be concerned, if that's what's bothering you."

Eli smiled. He was really out of practice. The girl was able to see through his crude interrogation immediately and hoisted him up on his own petard. He would have to try at another time, when she was less guarded and more open. If that time ever came.

"Don't worry, I'm just curious. So, that much work must keep you pretty busy. I'm surprised a beautiful woman like you isn't totally occupied just managing her social life."

She frowned a bit but remained upbeat. "I'm afraid you have the wrong impression about me, Eli. You're male chauvinism is showing. But if you must know, I don't feel bad about my life – in any case, most *men* don't really know how to handle me. I don't really have much time for a social life with my schedule. When you've a business to run, it's pretty much a 'round the clock operation."

"Sorry about that. I didn't mean anything by it. So there is no "Mr. Right" in your life?"

"No," she chuckled, relaxing. "My white knight must be riding a very slow horse." They both laughed and the tension eased perceptibly. Eli let up a bit on the accelerator and relaxed his grip on the steering wheel.

The sun was already sliding low along the mountains as the little car inched its way up towards

San José, and long shadows filled the valleys and cooled the evening air. Traffic had been amazingly clear right up until they hit the outskirts of the capitol. Mai Lee dozed off as the sun set, her head tilting slowly from side to side as the car swayed around the hills. They had the good fortune to be blessed with a full moon to light the darkened highway, and it filled the night sky over San José like a huge, dull orange sun. The vacant orb hovered over the volcanoes and cast an eerie glow on the valley below. San José glittered that night as if the sky had been turned upside down, a million shiny jewels sparkling against the amorphous black background of the volcanoes. The view was hypnotic at times, and Eli found himself fighting back fatigue as they entered the city.

"Eli, where are we now?" she mumbled, still groggy from her nap.

"San José. We're going to see a friend, someone I can trust. He'll put us up for a day or two until we can arrange to get out of the country unnoticed. Relax for now - I'll wake you up when we're there." The girl had already lapsed back into a light sleep, her head bobbing limply. Her smooth, jet-black hair fell like a curtain in front of her face and swayed gently as Eli piloted the Tercel around the streets of the quiet city. He turned down *Avenida Central* and searched for that building number he knew so well, the one with the familiar *façade* where Max would be waiting. Now, Eli would have to test their long-standing friendship to the limit.

"Mai Lee, wake up. We've arrived." Eli touched her

shoulder slightly and she sat bolt upright, looking quickly at the new surroundings.

"Yes, yes, I'm sorry, Eli. I haven't slept well lately and I...."

"Save it," he interrupted. "I've been there a few times myself." Eli jumped out of the car and pulled his bag out through the open window. "Let's get moving so we can hide this piece of crap car." Mai Lee followed him up to the storefront with her small suitcase swinging from side to side. "Ah, Max," Eli said out loud, "you just won't fix the damn place up." The sign read, "Max Gutierrez - European Shoes," and Eli rang the dirty door bell several times with gusto, glancing at the upstairs window for signs of life. A dim light finally went on in the apartment, and two voices began to chatter away in Spanish.

"What do you want?" Eli's friend called down without looking out the window.

"What do I want? Max, it's me, Eli. Open the door." A flurry of muffled shouts and bumping noises signaled a stumbling descent down the stairs. A small light went on in the back of the shop, and Max appeared at the door. He was dressed in the same old "Welcome to Miami Beach" T-shirt and shorts Eli had last seen him in, souvenirs of his only trip there with Eli. Max's tousled gray hair was a mess, and he stared quickly through the window at Eli before he opened the door.

Max grabbed Eli in a warm bear hug and smiled. "Brother, how are you? What brings you to.....?" He paused when he saw Mai Lee, and quickly ushered the two inside. They went upstairs immediately without exchanging another word, and he put down the window shade to obscure his visitor's presence. "Eli, who is the doll?"

"Max, let me present Mai Lee Jones. She's a friend."

"Very much a pleasure to meet you. Any friend of Eli's is a friend of mine. You are welcome in my house."

"Thank you," replied Mai Lee. "That's very kind of you."

Eli embraced his friend again and they both smiled. "It's been a long time my friend, a long time." Eli looked him over quickly and laughed. "I see you still know a good meal when you see one, *gordito*."

Max laughed and rubbed his ample stomach with a sweep of his hand. "*Si, amigo*. What is it I can do for you?"

"Max, we need some help getting out of the country without attracting any attention. We've had some trouble already – some bad guys at Playa Coco. We need to lay low until the San Francisco flight tomorrow and find a way to get the bad guys off our tails. Give us a head start, you know."

"*Si,* my friend, I know what you mean." Max fingered his thin mustache and stared at the floor, lost in thought.

"I have an idea I'd like to bounce off of you - maybe you can come up with the resources to make it happen." Eli patted his old friend and partner on the back and smiled. "What do you think?"

"*Si,* Eli, I will help. First, did you eat?" He turned to his wife and motioned for her to go to the kitchen. "You will eat first, and then we can talk. I will hide the car now." The rotund little guy threw on his torn terry cloth robe and started for the door. He glanced at the girl and said, "Please, be at home here. Relax and be comfortable. *Señorita*, please go with Rosa. She will help you with your things."

"Thank you again," said Mai Lee as she followed the older woman up the stairs.

"The facilities are through that door," Eli called out to Mai Lee as he followed Max down the stairs. They walked through the shop in darkness and Eli stopped his friend before he ventured outside. "When you come back, we have to talk about my guest. I don't trust her, so you need to be careful."

Max nodded slowly and answered, "No problem, my friend." He slipped quietly through the front door and quickly drove the little Toyota around the block and out of sight. A minute later, he casually approached from the opposite direction, and darted back inside.

They sat in a darkened corner of the shop, surrounded by cheap imitation leather pumps with stiletto heels. The smell of vinyl was nearly overpowering, and Max must have sensed the same thing, for he reached up and flicked on a small ceiling fan. "Max, this girl hired me to do a job, but the bad guys have already made both of us. And that's just the start. I'm sure we've been followed, at least as far as the city, but I can't tell how much she knows. She's either part of something really strange, or she's telling me the truth."

"*Si*, that is a problem. What do you wish to do?"

"Well, regardless of who is following us, we need to make them go away. Would you like to guess how we're going to do this?"

"You know, my friend, when I saw you at the door with that chick, I knew that you wanted more than a bed to sleep in." His smile was lit eerily by the faint streetlights of *El Centro*, flashing off his solitary gold tooth. "Ok, tell me what you are thinking."

"Here's the plan. Since we can't exactly make our unseen friends go away without a reason, we'll just give them one. Take the car and our papers out to Turrialba, you know, that place where the road winds sharply through the mountains. Toss in a couple of bodies and send it over the side."

"I think I can do that," he smiled.

"I thought you could, old friend, but I'm afraid to ask these days."

"*Si*. I have a friend at the city hospital. He will return the favor he owes to me." Max leaned his round stomach toward Eli in an effort to whisper. "You will not be disappointed."

"I knew I could depend on you, just like always." Eli smiled and patted his friend's shoulder. "Now we better get back upstairs before my little guest gets suspicious."

They climbed the stairs quickly and went to the kitchen in time to help carry the food to the table. Mai Lee and Eli ate the *morros y chiros* and *platanos* hungrily but silently, and didn't stop until they'd eaten all Rosa had prepared. Max led his confused wife away for a private word while their hungry visitors finished. She returned a few minutes later without him, wearing a bright polyester house dress and an equally artificial smile.

Max whisked past us just long enough to excuse himself. "I have to go now. I will see you later." He smiled and kissed Mai Lee's hand. "*Señorita*, please excuse me."

Mai Lee smiled, a bit embarrassed, and said, "Where is he going?"

"He has a few things to run down for me before we leave. Don't worry. Max is the best man I know at tying up loose ends." Mai Lee drank down her *Nehi* soda and relaxed back into her shaky chair. Rosa emerged from the kitchen and, observing the tired state of her guests, began to clear the table. "Rosa, let us," said Eli smiling. "Remember, clothes and papers," Eli reminded her softly. She gasped at her lapse in memory and nodded quickly, shuffling off to the bedroom.

"What did you just say to her?" demanded Mai Lee. Her unusually light eyes bored holes straight through Eli, probing for the truth in his answer.

"I just told her that she needed to remember that we needed some new clothes and identity papers." Eli realized that his lack of trust in the girl would make their escape more difficult than he had anticipated. "Besides, you look like you could do with a few hours sleep, anyway. It will take until later tonight before we're ready to move again, so let's make the most of it."

"Yes, of course," she replied quietly. They cleared

the table and pulled out the old folding couch in their host's bedroom.

"You take the bed; I'll take the chair," said Eli. Mai Lee ignored him and moved to arrange the chair cushions to suit her.

"I appreciate the gallantry, Eli, but there is no need for you to treat me like a defenseless female. I'm perfectly capable of taking care of myself."

"Forget it," he shot back, pushing past her. "When we get to Hong Kong, we'll need your wits sharp and ready. You take the bed." She thought for a second about protesting, but was too tired to fight about it. She stretched out on the bed and propped up the cushions to serve as pillows.

"Tell me how you met Max," she said as Eli tried to get comfortable. "How did you get into this line of work?"

"Look, we need to get some sleep," Eli admonished.

"Please," she whispered sleepily.

"Sorry – not part of the job. I'll keep that to myself."

"Really Mr. Rose! I was hoping you wouldn't turn out to be such a bore." Mai Lee's eyes were at half-mast and her lithe body sagged into the bed. "Why are you here, in this place? Why were you in that god-forsaken hole of a town?"

"We can discuss that some other time," he said.

The girl's eyes were shut, so Eli pulled the covers over her gently and continued. He turned out the small lamp and sat back in the chair, comforted by the security the dark room offered. Once Eli could be sure which side of the fence she was on, or he at least could make a confident guess, he'd be more truthful with her. But as long as they were being watched that was impossible. There was only one way to disappear into the background, one way to be sure that they could throw off the scent of their shadowy pursuers. It seemed perfectly clear to Eli, and he was almost surprised she hadn't just guessed his plan outright. Clearly, they both had to die.

Chapter 3

"Eli, Eli, wake up!" Max shook Eli so hard it felt like his head was going to fly off. Eli's senses returned quickly in the brightly lit room.

"Yeah, I'm Ok - Lord I'm stiff. Hey! What's up?"

"Everything is ready." He glanced around the room as Eli attempted to stretch the kinks out of his back. "Where is the girl?"

"She's not in the shop?" said Eli with a sinking feeling. The possible complications her disappearance would create drove Eli into a frenzy, and he frantically mulled over his options. That she was off to advise her compatriots was a very real possibility, and Eli felt like an idiot for falling asleep and ignoring her. "Never mind, *amigo*. We'll worry about her later. Give me the details and tell me what you want me to do."

"All is ready. Rosa will be coming soon with the papers, and you will leave tonight for San Francisco." He reached into the pocket of his windbreaker and pulled out two well-folded coach-class tickets. "Before you go to the airport, there will be a terrible accident.

Such a shame. On the television tonight and in the newspaper, there will be a story about two foreigners that have been killed in the mountains. When people go to identify the bodies, you will already be on the airplane. What do you think?"

"Sounds smooth *amigo*, very smooth. I just hope it buys us the time we need. Now, you didn't use live ones for this, did you?"

"Trust me, my friend," he smiled wryly. "Remember, I have many friends in high places that have helped. Do not consider the source."

Eli hoped he had used cadavers from the morgue at the city hospital as he'd promised, and not made some last minute substitutions with any of the anti-government crowd. "Whatever you do, you have to tell Violeta the truth. I don't want her thinking the worst."

Max patted Eli on the shoulder. Eli winced slightly, still feeling the bullet he took from Jasper so many years earlier. Although the wound had healed, Eli's psyche was still damaged. Maybe it didn't really hurt, but he felt the pain nonetheless. "Do not worry," Max replied. "I will tell her personally. That way she will be Ok."

"Thanks." Eli smiled and refocused on his new problem. "We need to find the girl, *pronto*. Otherwise she'll blow the whole thing. Let's go." They were headed downstairs when the shop door opened and Rosa and Mai Lee shuffled in, their arms laden with grocery bags.

"Oh, Eli. So glad you're up. Be a good chap and give us a hand with these, please." She extended a bag toward Eli, and he and Max carried the load up to the cramped little kitchen. Mai Lee smiled at Eli smoothly, and flashed her fiery blue eyes. His skin tingled even though he was furious with her for having gone out.

She began to unpack the bags as though nothing out of the ordinary had occurred, carefully handing cans to Rosa to store in their proper niches. "Had a good morning?" Eli said sarcastically. "Do you realize how dangerous it was for you to go out? What if you'd been spotted, or worse?" he said, exasperated.

"How stodgy," she pouted, unconcerned. "I was only trying to do something for our gracious hosts."

Rosa and Max were chatting quietly near the kitchen door, and the old woman slowly reached into her bag and pulled out a small parcel. Max turned to Mai Lee and offered, "Rosa says that she is very grateful for this gesture, as am I." He smiled, but the effort was strained.

"You see," said the girl defiantly, "they appreciate me, even if you don't."

Eli grabbed her arm sharply, intending to snap her out of her smug mood. "Look, you just don't get it, do you? Well let me spell it out for you - there are some pretty bad people out there trying to find us and you just might have given them all the opportunity they needed. I'm real sorry if this puts a cramp in your style but don't move, don't even piss again without asking me first. Got it?"

Mai Lee was stunned by Eli's verbal attack and stared at him silently for a minute. "Mr. Rose," she began cautiously. "Please don't forget who is paying you. I'll thank you to mind your tone." She glared at him and forcefully pulled her arm away.

They stared at each other for a few uncomfortable seconds before Eli, still staring into those fiery blue eyes said, "Max, is everything ready?"

Max nodded and handed Eli the parcel, and he sat down on the sofa and began to sort through the contents. Two worn but real U.S. passports, some tourist-type photographs of the countryside, some keys, and social security cards. The girl turned away silently and continued to help Rosa with the groceries. Eli called out for her to join him on the couch, and she approached hesitantly. "Take this stuff and memorize what's on it."

"What's this?" she asked meekly.

"Wrong question," said Eli curtly. "What you should be asking is, who's this?" Eli opened the front cover of the passport to her picture, which had been expertly copied. "Mai Lee Jones, meet Jane Hunt, happily married San Francisco homemaker. You have two wonderful young sons, Jeffrey and Edward, a large house in the Marina district, a maid, and a white pure-bred poodle named Antoinette."

She stared at him, dumbfounded. "Oh, I see." She paused. "And I suppose you are Mr. Hunt?"

"At your service, my love." Eli smiled sarcastically.

He lowered his tone and continued, trying to defuse the tension between them. "These are the children." He put the photo of two sweet-looking boys playing in a field on the sofa beside Mai Lee. "Study your passport, the pictures, the whole lot. Make sure you know which countries you've visited, when, and why. Know where you live, what the neighborhood is like, who your mother and father are, everything. We can't afford any mistakes."

"Really, Eli, do you honestly believe this is necessary?" She looked forlornly at the pile of papers and back at Eli, but he persisted.

"We came to Costa Rica on a sightseeing trip, and now it's back to the kids. Our connecting tickets to Hong Kong will be waiting at the airport in San Francisco." Eli held up a locker key to illustrate the point. "We'll pick them up at one of our less-used drops...... Remember, no mistakes." Her attention drifted so Eli sighed audibly to attract her gaze. "Listen, please. I know this is a pain, but you really do have to do this, and you have to get it right."

"Why? I'm not convinced that any of this is really necessary. We've gotten away from those thugs......... How can you be so sure we're being watched?"

"Trust me," Eli said sarcastically. "I've done this kind of crap a couple of times so I think I have a pretty good idea what that stuff at the Ocotal was all about. We're dead, get it. Killed outside Turrialba in a fiery car crash. If those goons from the Ocotal or their bosses think we're still alive we really will be here forever."

Max nodded his affirmation, and Mai Lee said, "Alright. I'm sorry I've been so stupid. Of course I'll do as you say, but would you mind first if Rosa and I run to the druggist for a bit? There are a few things I absolutely must have before this trip."

"What? Look, Rosa can get the stuff by herself, or

you can get it in San Francisco." Eli was irritated that his admonishments had been ignored but tried to let it pass quickly. "We have three hours, just three more hours 'till we're out of here. I suggest you pass on the druggist and get started with this stuff. Make a small list of your absolute necessities, and I'll get Rosa to pick the stuff up for you."

"Yes, of course," she said softly. If Eli had been just a little less paranoid, he would have said his employer was actually heartbroken about it. The tall beauty sat back on the beaten old sofa and began to study the passport, examining the pages slowly.

Eli walked over to Max and whispered "Perfect as usual my old friend. Just like the old days." He grinned and gave Max a small hug. "Send the bill to our *amigos* at Langley and put Ollie North's old handle on it. That'll shake 'em up."

"*Si,* brother, but you must be careful, Ok? Something is not right with this – I can feel it here." Max clapped his meaty palm to his ample chest. He always could smell a skunk in the next district, and Eli knew he was right.

"I hear you, buddy, but I want to play this hand out. If this works we'll be back in business again, *si*?"

Max hesitated and glanced at the floor, uncharacteristically quiet. "Eli, this place is quiet. I like my life now. No guns, no devils to deal with. I think maybe I don't want to go back to the old ways." He stared into Eli's eyes and Eli knew he was sincerely opting out, whatever the future brought.

Eli chose to ignore him, for now. "Is everything else ready? You have a car for later?"

"*Si,* brother. My son Juan will take you, and he also has your luggage."

"Perfect." Eli thought for a minute and said, "I need you to take a letter to Violeta for me when I've gone, when you go to tell her the truth. Please be certain she gets it."

"You have my promise. I will give it to her myself."

Eli sat at the kitchen table and tried to write something meaningful on the paper, something that might explain or excuse his sudden absence. Despite the risk of losing his cherished adopted family he realized that living a quiet life by the beach wasn't the solution to his problems by any means. The drinking, the gambling, his unwillingness to do anything constructive were just ways for him to bury the pain of his past. But now that familiar old fire had awakened in him again after a five year sleep, and he knew he must follow a new path. That path led to a second chance, and Eli realized he could never go back to Violeta's peaceful little cottage again.

He frowned, knowing that he had to make this choice. The metallic-cold taste of danger was back, and Eli was once again like a smack addict on a good ride. He knew this day could come again, the day he might turn his life upside down and go back to his old ways. *There must be something wrong with me*, he thought, putting the pen down and rubbing his forehead. *I must be crazy to want to go back to this life.* All those years of government work had changed him from the idealistic and eager agent he was in 1970 to the cynical and cold person he'd become. But he never saw it coming. *The change must have been gradual,* he thought, *but the straw that broke the camel's back was Managua.* Maybe if he started over he could chase away those demons and finally live with his past? Another chance to right those wrongs and move on with his life.

It wasn't artful or very inspiring, but the note said enough about the way Eli felt to make Violeta understand. He'd left women before of course, but it had never hurt, not like this. Eli hoped he'd said enough he to satisfy her tears. He hated to hurt her, but to save himself, to save his sanity this was the way it had to be. Eli folded $5000 into the envelope, pressed it to his lips and sealed it tightly.

§

"Slow down, *niño!*" Juan smiled and continued to drive frantically toward the airport, bobbing and weaving through traffic like a skilled boxer dodging a knockout punch. All of Eli's precautions could have proven useless in an instant, and he laughed to himself at the irony of dying in a traffic accident after all he'd been through. Eli and Mai Lee had said their good-byes to Max and Rosa and thanked them profusely for the help and hospitality. Eli promised to contact Max when he felt they were safely away and Max promised to tell

Eli of Violeta's reaction to the note. He smiled and gave Eli a huge bear hug when he'd seen the money in the envelope, then sent the travelers off with his oldest son to the airport at breakneck speed.

The terror of countless Latin American taxi rides was never lost on Eli, and this trip was no exception. Every ridiculously panicked trip to the airport deposited him at the end of one infinitely long, fossilized check-in line, where the security personnel scammed the rich *gringos* for bribes or just played out their *machismo* to boost their poor self images. But that was the way things limped along down south and you either got used to it or went crazy trying.

After Eli paid the departure tax he and Mai Lee shuffled into the first class cabin and settled in for the beginning of their odyssey. They had only a short layover in San Francisco before 16 non-stop hours to Hong Kong, a tough trip when you were rested and ready for it. Eli decided not to let his beautiful companion out of his sight for a second once they got to San Francisco. Their covers, maybe even their lives hinged on this unpredictable girl not blowing it. They sat silently as the big jet left Eli's adopted home and they continued that way for a long time afterwards. Eli wasn't in the mood for small talk, and deep and meaningful conversation didn't seem particularly worthwhile either. Planning strategy was his only concern. How he was going to avoid the bad guys and manage this Asian "unknown quantity" was his first concern. Hong Kong presented a more formidable challenge to him since his Cantonese was definitely not up to snuff. Mai Lee would be able to say anything to anyone without much concern of Eli knowing whether she was selling him out or trying to save him.

Eli continued to be puzzled by the whole affair. He had more questions than answers at this point. So Vicente had personally recommended him to the family. He could believe that, especially since he knew nothing of Vicente's whereabouts and activities since that last go-round with Jasper in Managua five years earlier. If that was the case, why did he feel so uncomfortable with the situation? Eli guessed it was because Mai Lee was clearly holding something back. But why? Was the attack at Ocotal really meant for her or for him? And if it was intended to dispatch him, why wait? Why not just ambush him while he was stumbling home after some drunken card game? Too many things didn't make sense, but he was too tired to unravel it all just now.

As if she'd been reading his mind, Mai Lee said, "Eli, we need to lay out a plan before our arrival in Hong Kong. I'm not actually very comfortable being left out of the decision loop, and I really think that..........."

"Don't worry," Eli interrupted. "That's your territory, your home turf. I'm going to need you to run the show in Hong Kong. I'll follow your lead for a change. How does that sound?"

"I was hoping you'd say that," she said smiling. "It

could have been quite difficult to convince you to go along with my plans, especially if I'd have had to have you locked up for a few days while I arranged everything. Now that won't be necessary." She pretended to read a magazine, but smiled broadly.

"That would have been positively dreadful!" said Eli, mimicking her accent. "And no way to treat a guest in one's home."

She smiled again and said, "Glad to see you have a sense of humor under all that Latin bravado. I was almost convinced you were one of those one-dimensional western brutes I so often meet."

""Well, I've been called worse. At least I try to be lovable and endearing, right?"

"That remains to be seen."

Thank God, Eli thought. *If the mood lightens a bit I might be able to get to the real story behind the story.* "Oh, really?" Eli asked. "Well I can do better."

"Hmmmm..........We'll see about that," she chuckled to herself. She gazed up at Eli while she continued to read.

"Really, once we get to your neck of the woods I'll follow like a lap dog, promise," Eli whispered.

She burst out laughing in short cascades but quickly regained control. "I can't believe that. We'll just have to see how it goes," replied Mai Lee, laughing again. Eli smiled and let it drop, and she went back to her magazine, chuckling softly to herself for a few seconds before finally settling in.

Eli knew that in Hong Kong he'd have to rely almost totally on her judgment, and he hoped her nerve was as resolute as her smile was beguiling. Eli dozed off, thinking of San Francisco and their tricky exit from the country.

Chapter 4

He slept for what seemed like seconds when a change in the tone of the engines signaled their initial descent into San Francisco. Eli awoke exhausted and with a stiff neck and a headache. Mai Lee had also drifted off, so he touched her shoulder lightly to wake her. "Mai Lee, we need to talk."

"Yes?" she whispered wearily. "Right, I'm sorry. I just dropped off for a few minutes. What shall we talk about?"

"Let's go over the drill in San Francisco. We can't afford any mistakes." Eli pulled out his passport and held it up to her, covering her name and address. "Ok, now who are we?"

She sneered a bit and said, "Fine. You are John Hunt, my husband.......And a damn cheap one, I might add."

"Ok, cut the sarcasm. What else?"

"We have two children, a neurotic dog, a maid, a nanny, and a large mortgage."

"A nanny?" I queried. "Where did the nanny come

from?"

"Well, you don't expect a woman of my background to manage that big house and those boys by myself, do you?" She smiled slyly, like a child testing the limits of her teasing.

"Of course not, dear," replied Eli wryly. "But let's try not to get too creative, Ok?" She nodded, wide-eyed. "Stay close after we hit the terminal. We'll find the locker, grab the bag, and check in as fast as we can. The objective will be to melt into the crowd quickly. The longer we take to do this, the more likely it is we'll be spotted."

"Spotted by whom?"

Eli shook his head in disgust, attempting to convince her that his patience had run out. "Look, I realize you're a novice at this but try to keep up, will you?" She nodded obediently again, but Eli wondered if it was all just an act. She just seemed too naive to believe.

"Just because we "died" in Costa Rica doesn't mean we fooled everyone. At this point we're just damn lucky. There's a better than average chance that we were spotted at the airport, and we could just as easily have a welcoming committee waiting at the gate for us when we arrive."

"Oh, I see........I'll try to keep up, Eli. I promise." She gestured a cross over her ample left breast with a well-manicured finger and smiled smugly. There was no question in Eli's mind that she was smarter and knew a lot more than she let on. It was to her advantage to make him think she was scatterbrained. Eli reasoned that underestimating this girl could lead to dire consequences for anyone, not just him.

"Keep in mind," Eli repeated, "that I killed a man back there defending us. I'm sure you don't believe that the people who sent those thugs will stop any more than I do." Mai Lee stared at him uncertainly and finally seemed to understand the gravity of the situation.

There was nothing about the girl that suggested to Eli that she was dimwitted, and he wondered whether she thought *he* was as stupid as she wanted him to think *she* was. As they got off the plane in San Francisco, Eli quickly grabbed her hand and said, "Ok, Mrs. Hunt, let's take a walk." Their entry through immigration went smoothly so they grabbed their faux luggage and checked through customs with unexpected ease. Eli pulled Mai Lee down the terminal towards the Hong Kong check-in area, searching all the while for a section of storage lockers that lined the wall near the gate.

"Over there," she called out, tilting her head towards the terminal entrance. They weaved slowly through the crowd of fretful travelers on their right and up to the storage lockers. Eli fumbled in his pocket for the key Max had given him back in San José. The number on the key was 1617; the locker opened, thankfully, without a problem. A small flight bag fell out of the narrow space and landed on Eli's shoe. Two new, large *Samsonite* bags lay under it, filled with clothes and bearing luggage tags with their assumed names and address. Eli smiled at the efficiency of it all, knowing just how much trouble Max and his old network of contacts must have gone through to make certain everything checked out right.

"What's so amusing?" Mai Lee asked.

"Nothing," Eli said with a satisfied smile. "You take the small bag and I'll take these two." They grabbed their new things and walked over to the United Airlines terminal, settling in behind an older couple with a matched set of Pierre Cardin bags. Eli grabbed the small flight bag from Mai Lee and pulled out two round-trip business class tickets. "Let me have your passport." She rifled through her purse and handed it to him, staring silently as if she were pouting. "Let me do the talking 'till we get out of here, Ok?"

"Yes, sir," she said with a salute and a smile.

The older couple finally managed to achieve their goal of adjoining seats and left contented. Eli threw their bags onto the scale and shoved the tickets at the attendant. "Hi, how're we doin' today. Two to Hong Kong with two bags to check." Eli smiled his most ridiculous smile in a feeble attempt to look like a tourist.

The young attendant took the tickets and passports without expression and began to enter the flight data onto his computer screen. "Mr. and Mrs. Hunt," he said without looking up. "Just the two of you traveling today?"

"Yep, just me and the Missus," Eli blurted out,

putting his arm around Mai Lee's waist and pulling her close. She forced a stiff smile and quietly stepped on his toe to signal her disapproval. "Yeah, it's like a second honeymoon for us without the kids." She mashed down harder on his throbbing toe as Eli tried to keep his composure.

"Well, Mr. Hunt, I hope the two of you have a good trip." He smiled dryly and handed the tickets and passports back, pointing down to his left. "That's Gate 18A, through the lobby and down to the left. Thank you for flying United."

"Thank you," Eli shot back. "Come on, dear," he said to Mai Lee, twisting her arm hard and pushing her towards the lobby. They walked through the concourse towards security, trying to avoid a hoard of vacationing Japanese tourists shuffling through in a chaos of bags and cameras. "You may or may not like the idea of our "arrangement," my love, but you damn well better start acting like you do."

"Or else....?" she added sourly.

"Or else nothing. I just drop you like a hot rock, love, and I fade back into the scenery. Look, you hired me to do a job and I'm doing it. Any time you don't wish to continue our agreement just say the word. I sure as hell don't need this gig."

"But you *do* need this gig Mr. Rose. You're the one who was barely scraping by in that little hole of a town. You're the one with the checkered past and the dim future. You've already burnt all your bridges, haven't you?" She stared at him coldly with the satisfied look of having made her point.

"Yes," Eli growled, "you got it right. But it's a big world and there's lots of opportunity out there, even for an old has-been like me. If you want to go this alone, be my guest. As far as anyone knows, I don't exist. I don't have anyone at the other end ready to look for me if I don't show up. This is your problem, honey, not mine. If you want to live through this and get that statue back you'll do things my way, at least until we get to your turf." He paused for emphasis and looked deep into her eyes. "Now do you want to do this or not?"

She pouted silently while they cleared the X-ray machine, and shuffled after Eli as he charged full-speed toward the gate. "Look, can you just stop ordering me around? I hate being ordered around....It reminds me of some bad times in my life."

"Sure," snapped Eli without hesitation. "No problem.....As long as you do what I say." She mumbled something under her breath and Eli said, "What's that?"

"I was just thinking how consistently boorish all men are. All you can do is order women about like they're little toys or something. Even Uncle wanted things done *his* way." She stood there gloomily, staring down the terminal and away from Eli.

"Well I've got some news for you, lady. We're not all the same, despite what you think. It's just your tough luck to be on the short end of it this time. Remember, you picked me, not the other way around. I'm sure Vicente had plenty to say to you and "Uncle" about how I go about my business." She wasn't too happy, but

Eli didn't care. He just needed her cooperation, not her friendship. "You'll get the chance to run the show soon enough."

They boarded the plane and stared out in opposite directions until well after they were airborne. Eli opened a magazine and pretended to be interested in the mildly entertaining contents, occasionally glancing in her direction but avoiding direct eye contact. When he'd finally cooled down enough to look directly over to her, the girl was bobbing and humming to her piped-in airline music, oblivious to the rest of the world. She frustrated him more than almost any other person he'd ever known but she continually drew Eli's gaze like a magnet. Again he found himself staring at the long expanse of smooth leg exposed by the slit in her black dress. His eyes hungrily followed the skin until it met the cold fabric barrier, and then skipped up to her shear silk blouse and the deep cleavage of her perfectly formed breasts. *Sure, she's beautiful*, he thought, *but business is business*. He refocused on the trip.

She must have sensed his gaze on her for she suddenly popped off her earphones and raised her eyebrows in anticipation. "Did you wish to say something to me? And please make it civil this time"

"Mai Lee, since we're going to be sitting next to each other for the next six hours or so, I don't want us to start this trip off on a sour note. I'm sorry I was so rough on you in the terminal," said Eli feeling short of breath. "You may not understand why I'm doing things this way so I'll try to lighten up a bit."

She smiled a beautiful, captivating smile, her full lips forming a smooth arc. "Apology accepted," she whispered. "I'll try and not give you such a difficult time from now on." She glanced away for a moment and then said, "Can you please tell me something more about yourself? I only know what Uncle has told me, those stodgy details about your mother and father and such." She leaned towards Eli, anxious and keenly curious like a school girl expecting her first kiss.

Eli sighed deeply, not wanting to say the wrong thing right away, but also not wanting to reveal too much. "Look, there's a lot I'd just love to tell you and maybe when we know each other a little bit better I'll feel comfortable enough to tell you more.....But not now."

She began to pout almost immediately. "You keep telling me that. How am I supposed to get to know you?" She gazed up at him with those blue eyes and he knew he was lost.

"Ok, I'll tell you a couple of things right now if you're truly interested." She nodded like a child so he continued, trying to reign-in his ego when too much detail crept out.

"I was involved in some fairly unusual goings on in Miami about 20 years ago. That's when I met Vicente Amarón, the man that recommended me to your uncle. We had some pretty wild times for awhile after that but things ended kind of suddenly about five years ago and we parted company. You already know from my bio that I ran a "consulting" business in Central America for the US Government for awhile, helping them with some odds and ends and "diplomatic" issues. I suppose I did Ok. People seemed to think I was the type of guy that could get results in a tight situation, so when I went back to Miami I did a few security-related jobs for some rich clients in need of discretion. The work paid well and wasn't too difficult, but circumstances brought me back to Costa Rica again and for the last five years I've been trying to enjoy the fruits of my labors."

Mai Lee chuckled and said, "The fruits of your labors? Looked more to me like you were hanging on by your fingernails."

"Well, in truth I guess the last couple of years have been a bit on the lean side." Eli smiled but felt the twinge of angst behind the half-truth of it. Old habits die hard!

"So why did you give it all up if you were so good at what you did?" she asked.

"Why? Yeah, well let's just say I took my own advice for a change and quit while I was ahead. Some things happened there at the end that didn't go well. I don't know." Eli sat back and remembered those last few days before he closed up the office and felt a small pain in the pit of his stomach. He should have refused that last job for Morgan. He knew it was too risky, going after Ortega and the Sandinistas with that traitorous team Morgan had recruited.

Eli knew the truth but had a hard time even admitting it to himself. He knew that he was no longer invulnerable and that his luck had only gotten him so far. The reality was hard to deal with but there it was in all its ugliness. What happened in Nicaragua had scared him out of the business. He survived it by sheer luck or good fortune, but he wasn't about to tell her that story.

"Did something bad happen to you? Was that it?" Eli was tired of her curiosity and decided to wrap up his impromptu biography quickly.

"Yeah, something happened that turned out bad for me and worse for others. It was one of those things that you don't get over easily, you know? But at the same time, I know I did the right thing. Anyway, that's my story or at least as much as I'm willing to tell you for awhile."

"I don't understand," she said, her eyes pleading for more detail. "I imagine that your line of work must have been very dangerous......" Mai Lee seemed excited by what he'd said, even though Eli hadn't provided any real details.

"Considering what happened at the Ocotal, that's something you should be personally acquainted with now," Eli interrupted. "I'm sorry," he added, just remembering his promise, "I did say that I wouldn't send any poisonous barbs your way, didn't I? Please forgive me."

"No, no, that's quite all right," she said wistfully. "Please go on, or at least tell me as much as you feel you can."

"There really isn't much more. Now you know firsthand just how dangerous this line of work can be. One can only do this job for so long before burn-out sets in."

"Or something else?" she asked.

"Or one becomes cold to it. That's probably the most dangerous part of it all, that you can become cold to the bad parts of the job. Someone I once knew taught me a valuable lesson about that, and I almost forgot it."

"Until that "thing" happened that forced you to quit. You must have been making a lot of money, so whatever made you stop must have been pretty awful." Mai Lee gazed at Eli like a small puppy looks at its mother, but he cut off the story without the finish she expected.

"Sorry, but that's it for this episode. All that is in the past and we're on to something new now."

"And if I hadn't shown up and ruined your tour business you would still be sitting in Costa Rica, happy in your retirement. I'm so sorry I mucked it up." She looked up at him and purposefully batted her long lashes a couple of times.

Even though he knew she'd done it on purpose it still aroused him. "Nonsense," Eli replied. "I was starting to get a little restless anyway. It was only a matter of time before the whole thing would have ended. I guess I'm just not the type of person that can settle down in one place permanently. That's one of my many character flaws." He lied, not wanting to tell her the real reason.

"Oh, I don't know," she purred. Those lovely blue eyes gazed at Eli with the same look he'd seen in Violeta's eyes many times before. Maybe he'd read the girl wrong?

"Well, regardless of the personality problems, here

we are. In my line of work it's not healthy to ask too many questions, so that's all you'll hear about my sordid life for awhile. But I'm not going to let you off the hook so easily. Since we're playing "true confessions" let's hear something from you."

She smiled almost coyly, but it looked disingenuous to Eli. She said, "Well, really, there's not much to tell."

"Ok. So fill in the gaps I don't already know. How does a woman your age end up running her uncle's business, especially in Hong Kong?"

"No sons," she shot back quickly, "and I don't *actually* run the business. Uncle does that quite well. I really just manage the financial end of things."

"Let's face it - He wouldn't have sent you after me if he didn't see you as his "Number One." You're his *Tai Pan*, and you know it."

"Perhaps," she chuckled with pride. "You know much more about how we do things than I thought you did. It is possible that Uncle relies on me to do a number of sensitive things. That hasn't always been easy in Hong Kong, as you have no doubt surmised." She paused for a second, introspectively silent, and stared out the window at the darkening sky. Her face saddened visibly for a moment, as if she were reflecting on some past loss. "You know, Uncle has been both mother and father to me since my own parents died. I owe him everything, more than you can ever imagine. I would do anything for him, anything he asks." She looked intently into Eli eyes, and he felt a coldness in her she'd kept well hidden until then. He was caught off guard by her stare, and he wondered just how many other things he'd managed to miss while he was staring down her dress.

"Yes, I'm sure you would," Eli said slowly, breaking the silence. "Was it your uncle then who sent you to England for your education?"

"Yes. He felt I should receive a proper education, grounded firmly in business and negotiations. After England, I returned to the firm as an inventory specialist and worked my way up from there."

"Sounds like it was a tough road," Eli said. "I'm surprised your uncle didn't start you in some kind of executive position."

Mai Lee smiled and added, "Uncle believes you cannot possibly understand a business unless you begin at the bottom. He has often repeated to me a favorite saying: every healthy tree has a good strong base from which to grow. In retrospect, I would have to agree."

"So there was a time when you and your uncle didn't particularly see eye to eye?" Eli asked, attempting to read between the lines.

"Did you always agree with everything your mother or father told you?" she shot back calmly.

"*Touché.*"

She paused for a moment and reflected on the thought. "Of course, we have disagreements even now but they are usually philosophical rather than operational."

Eli frowned at the coldness of her reply. Her analytical answers to his questions were largely devoid of emotion, and that made him very uncomfortable. This was in sharp contrast to her obvious flirtations and it left him confused again about how to read her. He changed the subject. "Well, with all the responsibility you have, you must meet a lot of very interesting men. Is there.....?"

"Someone special?" she interrupted briskly. "My, you certainly haven't mastered the art of subtlety. Remember, we already covered that aspect of my life." She calmed almost immediately, regaining her composure with lightening speed. Her wide eyes narrowed a bit and she smiled to herself. "Alright, if you insist. Yes, there was someone once. But nothing lasts forever and neither did our relationship. Does that make you happy?"

"Hey, I'm sorry lady. I didn't mean to touch such a sensitive nerve. I only wanted to check on the competition, knowing of course that there may never be an opportunity to........."

"My, my," she broke in again. "Don't we have a high opinion of ourselves?" She smiled and averted her gaze for a second. "But one never knows about these things." She touched Eli's thigh with a wispy stroke of her index finger and drew her luscious tongue slowly across her full red lips.

They laughed spontaneously, and she slapped his leg sharply. "I think I'm beginning to understand you a little better," Eli said. *It may be a put-on*, he thought, but Eli still felt that zing of anticipation that comes from the chance of a relationship with someone new.

"Perhaps you are," she laughed. "But you've managed to sidetrack my original question about your background pretty well. Now that I've shown you mine,

I'd like you to show me yours. Tell me again why you abandoned the high life in Miami for that Costa Rican backwater I found you in."

"Jeez, you ask a lot of questions for a properly educated Chinese girl," Eli mused. "All I'll tell you is more of the same. It was a personal choice, nothing more."

She pouted again and turned away in mock disdain.

"You still don't trust me, do you? Someday I hope you will."

"One never knows about such things. How about we both give up the cross-examinations and talk about the plan in Hong Kong?"

"Good suggestion," she added. "Hong Kong is my game, all the way. Kai Tak is a crazy place, so you should stay close to me. We'll get a limo and dash over to a hotel for the night. We can meet Uncle the next morning."

"Sounds pretty simple."

"'Tis," she chirped, and returned to her magazine with a self-satisfied look.

The hours dragged by like molasses in a blizzard. Eli remembered how painful all the other miserable trans-Pacific flights he'd ever taken were. He got up to stretch and try and stay awake, hoping some sort of activity would help hold back the waves of exhaustion that were sweeping over him. The rest of the passengers were scattered about in various states of disarray, and the whole lot looked like a group of displaced refugees rather than upscale travelers. Fourteen hours in a confined space can reduce civilized discourse into a series of polite grunts and gruesome bodily noises. Eli marveled at the thought of how loosely humanity was bound by its social mores, and how quickly those taboos would re-appear once they had landed. Mai Lee had slipped off to sleep for an hour or so, and Eli must have dozed too, for they were both awakened by a stewardess serving a late-night snack. The pitch and speed of the plane changed noticeably, indicating their approach into Kai Tak International Airport.

The giant 747 swayed slowly past the neon of Kowloon, delicately avoiding the series of apartment houses that lay along the flight path. They dropped in amongst the apartments as the ocean rose up to meet the jet, so close Eli could see laundry on the railings and televisions lighting up darkened rooms. A few moments later came the comforting thud of the landing gear meeting the asphalt of the runway, and they taxied briskly to the terminal. Mai Lee grabbed Eli by the arm as they trudged wearily off the plane and said, "Come with me, quickly." They dashed off to immigration in a vain attempt to slip by before the rest of the plane reached them, but found the lines already 15 deep with the passengers from two other flights. Mai Lee cursed and said, "Give me your passport." Eli handed it over, and she added, "Wait here 'till I tell you different." The girl paraded to the front of the line and waved over one of the inattentive-looking young guards. She whispered a few things in Cantonese to him, shoving the passports at his face insistently for emphasis. He nodded curtly and took the passports to the nearest booth where the resident agent protested, but stamped them. Mai Lee waved at Eli to join her, and they ran off to claim their bags.

"He is the cousin of a friend of mine," she explained as they grabbed the nearly empty bags. "She owes me a few favors, but now she owes me one less and now one to him."

"Very effective," said Eli. "So it helps to have friends here?"

"Cousins," she corrected. "It helps to have cousins."

The pair queued up for the friendly customs man and expected another long wait but Mai Lee soon spied a friendly face and ordered, "Come with me, quickly." They pushed their way through the mass of humanity trying to exit the building as if they had already cleared customs and she smiled at the guard as they passed. "Always go for the green line," she said. "It's usually faster, and even more so when your cousin is working the station." Eli smiled at the guy as they left the building and emerged at the curb. "There's one," she said, pointing at an unoccupied limo. "Let's get it, quickly." She secured the driver while Eli stumbled after her with the baggage. The obliging driver loaded them into the Mercedes while they escaped the madness in the leather-lined back seat. "That was easy," she exclaimed with a look of satisfaction.

"Yeah, a real snap," Eli added sarcastically. "Ok boss, it's your show and you've made a believer out of me. Lead on."

"Hong Kong Hotel," she snapped at the driver. He nodded silently, and they sped off into the rainbow shades of neon known as Hong Kong.

Chapter 5

Lack of sleep had a deadening effect on Eli's senses, but the vividness of the city infused him with a burst of energy. The streets bustled despite the lateness of the hour, overflowing with shoppers and restaurant-goers. Neon flashed, crowds surged, and the traffic snaked along the narrow streets. Each new turn exuded exotic sounds and smells from all sides, a nearly overwhelming cacophony that was at once intimidating, vibrant and exciting. "I do love it so," sighed Mai Lee quietly. "No matter what happens, my heart will always remain here."

"I can understand why," said Eli half-heartedly. They arrived at the hotel quickly and were ushered to the desk by the smiling doorman. The charming desk attendant checked them in rapidly and they were soon rushing off through the crisp lobby to the elevator bank. It had been many years since Eli had felt the understated elegance of such a place, which he decided was indeed more appealing than anything he'd seen in Costa Rica.

"I prefer to stay here rather than the Peninsula," said Mai Lee, noticing his examination of the lobby. "Too ostentatious for my tastes."

"Oh, I agree," Eli said with a touch of sarcasm. He did agree, however, especially since the hotel and shopping complex to which the Hong Kong Hotel belonged, the Ocean Terminal, was also a main ferry station. They could get to Hong Kong Island or Shenzhen in the morning with little inconvenience, and after traveling for 24 hours, that sounded pretty good to Eli.

"Two beds?" Eli asked as they entered their nicely appointed suite.

"We may be Mr. and Mrs. Hunt by day, but that is where the charade ends," she said with a smile. "For now......."

"Lord above, there's still hope," Eli laughed. She chuckled and closed the door. "Listen, I need to wash the last two days off my aching back and get some rest. You want to go first?"

"Well, I need to make a few calls first, so why don't you go ahead." She sat down on the bed and pulled an address book from her purse. Eli nodded and turned the hot water full on, fogging the bathroom like it was his private sauna. He let the water beat down on his aching neck and shoulders until he was nearly drowned, as if he was trying to wash away the previous five years more than get clean from the trip. There was a lot to wash off. It felt like a fresh start, one he didn't even realize he'd needed until it was already happening. Now all he had to do was keep it going. But nothing lasts forever, and Eli knew this job wouldn't be any different than all those that came before. When it all finally ended, then what?

Eli grabbed a terry cloth robe from the towel stand and wrapped himself in its warmth. "Ok, it's all........." His words trailed off when he realized that his lovely companion was gone. There was no note, no word of any kind. Eli walked out onto the veranda and gazed out at Victoria Harbor and the thousands of brightly lit little vessels bobbing about in the night. He felt once again that he'd been stupid and let his guard down. Now it seemed like he'd made a big mistake taking the job in the first place.

Eli remembered the last thing Vicente had said to him before he was marched into the Coast Guard station: "My son, now is the time for you to turn you disadvantage to advantage. Control the situation; no let the situation control you, and all will be Ok." The message had dimmed but Eli still remembered it. He'd committed what Vicente would have considered to be a cardinal sin, though it had almost taken him too long to recognize it.

He stretched out on one of the beds and studied a picture of Guilin that hung on the opposite wall. The towering, fog-shrouded peaks rested like silent sentinels while birds sang and nested in the trees below. Two wise men sat near a small shrine in the foreground contemplating the nature of man, Eli presumed. He smiled at the irony of the scene, so placid and tranquil, while the reality of China was so different. He drifted off to sleep.

Mai Lee returned after two in the morning and showered as quietly as she could. The running water woke Eli and he lay there in the dark, wondering if he should confront her with his misgivings. She crept quietly into the darkened room when she'd finished, turned down the covers on the other bed, and slipped in. Her long black hair was wrapped in a towel, and the neon of the city lit her in dim pastel hues. Eli was transfixed by the shape of her form beneath the single sheet she'd pulled across herself. Her perfect lines flowed so smoothly, one to the other. He couldn't imagine a more precisely designed work of art or nature, and it was difficult to maintain the guise of being soundly asleep. She tossed around for a bit and then got up and went to the open window. The lights shown through her sheer nightgown and illuminated her right side with a soft glow. The vision of her smooth skin in the cool evening air through that sheer fabric was more than enough to drive Eli insane. He closed his eyes, hoping it was a dream, but she was still there when he looked back.

She moved away from the window after what seemed like an eternity and climbed back into bed. Eli's pounding heart finally began to slow and he again tried to focus his thoughts on the picture of Guilin. Some artist could just as well have painted his idea of the perfect female form and brought it to life in the bed next to him, he decided. He turned over and tried to recall Vicente's warning once again, but all he could think of was the evening light bathing the girl's lovely body. Maintaining his composure and professionalism would have to wait until morning. He hoped he wasn't falling for her.

§

"Good morning, sleepy head." Eli opened his eyes, groggy from the jet lag, and saw the smiling face of his boss two inches from his own. "It's time to rise and shine. Make some hay, catch the worm and all that rubbish," she said shaking him. "I've got a proper English breakfast on the way up, so get dressed."

Mai Lee was wearing a conservative black business suit and had piled her hair up in a bun on the back of her head. Eli had slept in the bathrobe, and looked wilted and harried by comparison, "What time is it? He muttered.

"Seven," she replied cheerily. "Let's go, let's go. There is business to do today and much for you to learn."

"Sure boss lady," he answered gruffly. "By the way, where did you get the clothes?"

"Well I couldn't very well go to Uncle's dressed as I was so I slipped out last night and went back to my flat to get a few things. I also had some proper clothes tailored for you last night. You'll find everything hanging in the closet. I had to guess your sizes so I hope everything fits."

"Looks great from here," replied Eli. "You have a very good eye."

She smiled, looking self-satisfied for a change. "I also took the liberty of arranging our meeting as well, so we've got to get going."

Well that's at least one explanation for her vanishing act last night, Eli thought. A knock on the door interrupted her, and she added, "Now hurry up."

Eli dressed in the bathroom and admired the dark gray suit. It had been years since he'd worn anything like it, and it reminded him of his younger, more prosperous days in Miami. But the starched collar of the white shirt and the new burgundy silk tie felt restrictive after so many years of golf shirts or less. *Thank goodness the shoes fit*, thought Eli. He emerged to a plate full of fresh fruit, croissants, eggs and sausages, and blistering hot Chinese red tea and quickly devoured a croissant. "Well boss, what's the plan for today?"

"First, we catch the ferry to Hong Kong. A car will pick us up at Kennedy Road and take us off to Uncle's. I'll tell you the rest when we've had a chance to discuss it with him."

"So I finally get to meet the man himself."

She just smiled. "We'll leave the bags here. They will be delivered to us in Hong Kong with some new clothes and a few basic necessities. Right now we've got to run. Uncle does not like to be kept waiting."

"Charming," said Eli, swallowing a mouthful of tea. "Let's blow this place."

They caught the elevator to the shopping arcade level and strode quickly towards the ferry terminal. Few people were active at that hour of the morning, but the crowd began to grow as they reached the *Star Ferry* pier.

"Come quickly," said Mai Lee as they deposited the fare in the creaking turnstiles. "We must hurry to catch the 8 o'clock ferry. We mustn't be late. Uncle will not be happy if we're late, even by a minute." Eli shuffled off after her and was somewhat surprised to see a small crowd gathered at the yellow barricade that blocked off the dock. The sloping walkway pulled the two into the fray and soon they were squeezed in by those behind them, elbowing and jostling for positions close to the front of the line. "You see, there is no assigned seating so when the ferry master feels he is full, the barricade closes and you've missed your chance."

"Oh, I see," Eli replied in a matter of fact tone. It all brought back some not so fond memories of his previous experiences with Hong Kong crowds. At precisely 8 o'clock the barricade was lifted and the crowd surged forward as if Moses himself had parted the sea. The assembly gradually filtered off in different directions, quickly filling the colorful green and white boat with drab blues and grays. Mai Lee and Eli found seats forward, just behind the small wheelhouse so they could avoid the sea spray that always blew in off the rounded bow.

"As your host I feel somewhat guilty that we haven't more time to see the attractions of my city," she said quietly. "Unfortunately, this will have to do. This little trip affords one of the best views of the island available, so I do hope you'll enjoy the ride."

"I'm sure I'll enjoy it," Eli answered, "but I wouldn't be too concerned about my tourist interests. I didn't come here to see the sights and besides, this isn't my first trip to Hong Kong."

"Really? How interesting........I was under the impression that this was your first trip. Well then, all the more reason for you to leave with a favorable view. I hope the first was equally enjoyable?"

"Oh, yes," Eli added, "but the guide is so much more attractive this time." The girl smiled sweetly and stared out at the open water as the engines roared to life. The metal deck shook and vibrated and the ferry eased off the dock towards Victoria Harbor. Eli sat silently, taking in the view and recalling his past acquaintance with the city, when the atmosphere between the U.S. and China had not been quite as cordial.

Mai Lee talked about the city as they cruised slowly towards the massive glass and steel monoliths that passed for office buildings. Eli's mind wandered to other days, other places and he must have lost track of the conversation because the girl stopped in mid-sentence to get his attention. "Eli? Eli? You haven't heard a word I've said, have you?"

"Sorry. Must be the jet lag or something. What was it you were saying?"

"Over there, that big building with the gray glass is

Connaught Centre where our offices are located. You don't really care much about this, do you?" She looked at Eli sympathetically but he could tell she was a bit irritated.

"I don't mean to seem ungrateful," Eli replied apologetically, "but my mind isn't really on it right now. I'm a little more concerned with the job and getting to it."

The beauty averted her eyes and acted disappointed. "You don't find my company enjoyable?"

Eli touched her arm and brought her eyes up to meet his. "Of course I do but it's time to do some work, that's all. This business with your uncle is a formality I can live without." They stared off at the bow for a minute to watch a young English couple pose for a photo by the railing. Eli smiled at how simple their lives seemed from his perspective. It was an envious moment.

"This formality is more important than you can imagine," said Mai Lee slowly. "We both have much at stake here. Some things you already know and some you don't. You will find out today much of what you wanted me to tell you on the plane, many things I just couldn't tell you. Some details even I don't know."

Eli stared blankly at the girl and tried to convey with his expression just how tired he was of the game she was playing. Mai Lee looked away, preferring to watch the English couple rather than confront his anger. He knew there was more to the story than she'd told him, but now she knew he'd been on to her game all along and she was ashamed.........Or so he thought.

"Someday I'd love to play tourist like that," she murmured as the couple returned to their seats.

"Any place in particular?"

"Oh, I don't know," she answered wistfully. "Maybe someplace wild and without restrictions, like Nepal or New Caledonia, or Rio de Janeiro."

The ferry pulled in slowly and bumped the dock two or three times before the engines stopped. Mai Lee got up before the boat had stopped moving, and motioned for Eli to follow her. "Let's go." The small boat shifted noticeably to the right as the crowd swarmed over towards the exit. Eli's nerves started to twitch with concern that the old barge might capsize, and he looked around quickly for someplace safe to pull Mai Lee if the worst happened. She noticed his concerned look and grabbed his arm tightly. "Remember, this is Hong Kong." Eli shook his head and waited for the large metal gangway to drop onto the dock. The passengers streamed over the heavy metal walk like angry ants, wobbling slightly with the motion of the ferry until they had reached the concrete dock. Mai Lee kept a brisk pace out of the bowels of the ferry terminal, passing the rickshaw drivers that hovered nearby without acknowledgment.

Their trail led them past the giant office complexes of Connaught Centre, part of the essence of Hong Kong's commercial soul. Eli stared with amusement at the double-decker buses on Connaught Road Central, a vivid reminder of England's legacy. The streets and walkways surged with activity, a crush of humanity that never seemed to thin out. Smartly dressed office workers mingled at the walk lights with drably-attired shopkeepers and cooks. School children, wearing their starched and monogrammed uniforms congregated at the corners, waiting for the signal so they could cross. The aromas of a thousand *dim sum* shops flowed through the diesel fumes and enveloped everything in garlic-tinged air.

They crossed Queen's Road Central and began the steep climb up Garden Road to the Peak Tram entrance. "I could have had the car meet us here but when I thought this was your first trip, I decided you might rather see some of the more pleasant parts of the city this way." She surged past Eli to the ticket booth and had purchased them before he could even offer. The tram was just about to leave so they jumped on the last car and sat in the back. The steep angle of Victoria Peak produced the curious sensation of an off-balance ride, but the slow climb offered many pleasing views of the city and the small, secluded neighborhoods that populated the area. The tram reached the Kennedy Road Station quickly and the smartly attired couple walked out to find a large black Mercedes parked just outside the landing. A very large, formally dressed driver greeted Mai Lee and opened the door for her. "Good morning Baizhu. How is Uncle today?" she said.

"Fine, Miss. He waits for you and Mister at the house. We go very quick."

The massive guy powered the limo through the narrow, winding roads of Victoria Peak as if it was part of the asphalt and they soon arrived at a large pair of wrought iron gates. Eli made a mental note of the size of his hands as compared to the thin steering wheel. *Must have been a wrestler or something pretty nasty*, he thought.

Baizhu entered a seven-digit access code on a key pad in front of the entrance and the gates parted with slow severity. *So far, so good*, thought Eli. A seven digit key pad would present a real challenge to any professional trying to gain access to the compound. That was a sign that "Uncle" was focused on the details. *Very good, very good indeed.*

The house was shrouded by large flowering trees, and was not visible from the road. It sent a chill up Eli's spine because the place reminded him of another, very similar compound in Coconut Grove that he hadn't seen for many years. They roared to a stop in front of a pair of ornately carved teak doors and Baizhu hurried around to escort Mai Lee out of the car. Eli's brain began to replay events from his past as they approached the doors; the slight smell of mildewed wood and the damp feel of the place was eerily similar to the other house. His heart was pounding nervously and his palms were sweating just like they did in his youth at that old doorstep. They entered the stone walk and paused to ring the bell.

"Eli, are you feeling Ok?" asked Mai Lee observing his reaction. "You're looking a bit peaked."

"I'm fine," said Eli stiffly. He forced a smile and added, "Let's just get this over with." She rang the silent doorbell and the left-hand side opened almost instantly. The tiny old woman smiled when she saw Mai Lee and bowed slightly, greeting her by name. Mai Lee smiled and answered first in Cantonese, then in English.

"It's good to see you again, Arlene. Is Uncle on the terrace?"

"Yes Miss, and he has enjoyed his favorite breakfast this morning so I believe his mood will be good." The old woman smiled broadly, drawing out the deep furrows in her weathered forehead.

"Arlene, you're such a devilish thing. Thank you for setting him up for me." She bowed and walked through the spacious teak-paneled living room with Eli in tow. "She's been as close to me as my own mother these past few years," the light-eyed beauty said smiling brightly. They emerged from a set of French doors onto the open terrace, a semi-circular, stone covered veranda set down among the tops of the flowering trees. At one end of the terrace sat a bald little man in a high-backed wrought iron chair. He was staring down at the incredible vista of Victoria Harbor that burst through the trees, obscured only by the occasional low-hanging clouds or billowy wisps of ground fog that drifted by. He rose when he saw the pair and walked briskly but stiffly over to greet them. His crisply tailored suit fit him like a second skin, and Eli knew at once that he had imagined a completely different sort of man.

"My child," he beamed, extending his arms to embrace the beautiful girl. The old man hugged her warmly and said, "It's so good to see you back safely."

"It's good to be back, Uncle," replied Mai Lee with a genuine sigh of relief. "Please allow me to introduce Mr. Eli Rose, the man whom you wish to employ. Mr. Rose, this is my uncle, Mr. Cheung Lido."

"An honor sir," said Eli with a slight bow.

"For me as well, Mr. Rose," he replied, extending his hand. "Please call me Cheung. It is much easier." The old man eyed Eli up and down quickly, as if he was inspecting a horse. "I see you are somewhat familiar with our customs. That is good, a very good sign."

"Yes sir," Eli answered. "I'm sorry we're late - it was my fault. The jet lag caught me a bit off guard I'm afraid."

"Nonsense, don't worry about it," said Cheung. "Please, sit down. Would you have some tea?"

Eli nodded, and he and Mai Lee sat down across the small cherry-wood table from Cheung as he poured the aromatic brew into some fine China cups. "Mr. Cheung, I hope you will not consider it impolite but I would like to be brief. There are a number of things.........." The old man cut Eli off with a wave of his free hand while he poured the last of the tea. Cheung made a grand gesture of the whole action but Eli noticed that his hands remained steady throughout the procedure, like two rigid granite piers.

"I trust your trip went well?" he inquired with a raised eyebrow. "No problems, a smooth trip?" He handed Eli a cup and looked him squarely in the eyes.

"Yes, it went quite well I suppose, if you consider almost getting killed an integral part of traveling," Eli said dryly.

The old man smiled thinly and handed a cup to his niece. "You know, Mr. Rose, you gave me quite a fright when my sources in Costa Rica told me of my child's accident. It took me two days to find out that it was only a ruse to cover your departure from the country. I didn't actually know where the two of you were until Mai Lee telephoned me last night." He sipped his tea calmly, but was clearly annoyed.

Mai Lee smiled at Eli, as if to say "congratulations." Eli said, "I am sorry about that sir, but it was necessary to avoid some very nasty people who had some different ideas about our trip."

"Yes, Uncle," Mai Lee chimed in, "it was necessary. We had some difficulties in the town where I met Mr. Rose."

"Yes, I know," sniffed Cheung. He put down his cup disdainfully and frowned at the housemaid. "Please, Arlene, bring me something hot, not this cold dishwater." She bowed and quickly removed withdrew the teapot and cup. Cheung returned his attention to Eli and focused intently on his words." Now that you are here I hope to keep those kinds of incidents from occurring." He got up suddenly and walked briskly to the stone wall that overlooked the harbor. "So, Mr. Rose, you are wondering how I know so much about you and why I wish to employ you." He stood with his back to the seated pair, inhaling the cool air deeply.

"Well, actually I don't really care how you came to those decisions. Let's please cut the small talk and get down to business." Mai Lee gasped at Eli's unexpected breach of etiquette but Eli was tired of the facade that Cheung continued to maintain. He'd finally run out of patience and didn't want to be put on hold for even one more minute.

"Don't worry my dear," said her uncle calmly. He pivoted around and leaned back against the railing, smiling broadly. "He is right you know. My past association with Mr. Amarón should not be of any interest to him, but let's just conclude the thought by saying that it was indeed his recommendation that has resulted in your arrival here. So, we'll push on to our business."

Eli sipped his tea and watched Cheung closely, pacing in front of them in small arcs. Mai Lee gulped her tea and sat silently. Eli thought for a minute that she, too, was about to hear the complete story for the first time.

"Mr. Rose, what my niece told you about the carving we wish you to locate is true though there are a few more details that should be filled in before we discuss other matters."

"Something kind of told me that," Eli said bluntly.

"Yes," he sighed. "I'm certain you had some idea that there was more than what Mai Lee had told you. But in order for you to understand the difficulty involved in retrieving the item you must hear the entire story from the start." He paused and smiled as Arlene brought the fresh tea and replaced it on the table. She bowed curtly and left and the old man continued. "Many years ago," he said, gently fingering a small orchid, "Mai Lee's father and I began a long struggle against the Communists on the Mainland, chiefly against the forces of Mao Zedong. In point of fact, we fought against them on the side of the Nationalists until we had to flee here." He stared down at the bustling port, absorbing the view for a moment. "Although we were forced to leave our native land, we never lost hope and never gave up our struggle to live in a free China."

"Sounds familiar," said Eli, sipping his tea. "Please go on."

"For years we waged a silent but costly war with the Communists with the aid of several loyal compatriots inside the country. While little notice was taken of our efforts by the western press, the Mainland government certainly knew we were active. Let us just say, we had their undivided attention." Mai Lee stood up and begged a moment to make the upcoming travel arrangements. Cheung kissed her on the forehead and said, "This is the light that guides and strengthens me, all that keeps me upright. I'm sorry, where was I?"

"The Commies knew you real well............"

"Yes, yes," he said, walking to the brass rail again. "They knew us *very* well. But we wanted to attract the attention of the west to our struggle so we decided to do something spectacular, something the Communists could not hide. Something that would cause them much embarrassment.

Eli smiled wryly to himself, acknowledging the nature of such people. They all seemed to share a common gene – Julio, Vicente, even Jasper in his own twisted way. Idealists out to cause a stir and trumpet the cause. He understood the mindset, especially having felt that way himself for so many years. But Nicaragua broke him of that sentiment, his link to the "cause." And here he was again, with yet another patriot trying to save the motherland and punch up a vision that was impossible to recapture in the real world! No wonder Vicente had recommended him – he knew Eli would understand the old man's motivation, even if he could no longer believe in it himself.

"One of our loyal brothers learned of Mao's desire to expand his cultural ties with the west with the eventual hope, I suppose, of increasing trade or legitimizing his brutality. I'm not certain. He had decided to grant a request to send some of the precious treasures of Xian to a western museum for an exhibition, something that would be used internally and externally to promote the revolution. Many items had to be moved from several smaller regional museums to the vaults in the Forbidden City. Our brother also learned that among these treasures was a matched pair of jade carvings of Confucius, which Mao intended to unveil to the world as proof that a cultural rebirth was underway in New China. Some garbage about New China being able to coexist with the legacy of Old China." Lee grumbled and smacked his open palm on the railing. "We decided to unveil them in Hong Kong, instead." He smiled to himself and continued as Eli paid rapt attention. "I should never have assumed that *all* our comrades were as dedicated to the cause as Mai Lee's father and I. I never thought that self-enrichment would become a motive for some."

"Believe me, Mr. Cheung, I understand your frustration better than you know," Eli added bitterly.

"Quite," Cheung answered flatly. "With the aid of our compatriot Zhe Guoshi, who was a minor official in the Ministry of Culture, Mai Lee's father and I came into possession of the carvings. That was a great and joyous day for us." He leaned back, his eyes hollow and free of emotion. "However, before we could even leave China the Communists discovered our plot and captured us. The Red Guard took us to Guangzhou for interrogation. The Guard had been tipped off by Zhe, and he even joined them so that he could add his own "personal" touch to the proceedings. Our suffering was terrible but when they could not break us, they had Zhe transport us to the edge of the city near the Pearl River to be shot."

"So," said Eli slowly, "you managed to escape, but Mai Lee's father didn't?"

"No, Mr. Rose. Neither of us escaped, at least unscathed." He walked over to Eli slowly and pulled his shirt collar down around the back of his neck. An indentation that Eli recognized as a small caliber bullet wound was visible at the base of his neck near his spinal column. "I was lucky, Mr. Rose. The bullet pierced my neck near the spinal cord, but entered at a fortunate angle and exited my mouth. Mai Lee's father was less fortunate." He straightened his shirt and composed himself. "My best friend, my sister's husband was not as fortunate as I. Mai Lee was only an infant at the time and she had lost both parents, so I took her in and raised her as my own." The old man gazed out once more at the beautiful view below.

"They left us for dead. When I regained consciousness, I was in the hands of friends, on a sampan back to Hong Kong with my brother-in-law's body beside me."

Eli was stiff from sitting in the lightly padded metal chair so he walked over to look out on the tranquil scene below. "Mr. Cheung, maybe you can explain something to me. How did Mai Lee's father get into China in the first place? I mean, he was a *gwailo* wasn't he?"

Cheung chuckled and pulled the orchid from its precarious perch. "You really had to know Frederick in order to appreciate how talented he was. He was born in China – his father was an English missionary and his mother and I were from the rural provincial town of Kunming. He was as much Chinese as I am, maybe more so in some ways. We decided when it was time to go back that he would pass himself off as Uygur from Urumqi in Xinjiang Province. Many of those people have light hair and light eyes, you know. This seemed to satisfy everyone he came in contact with. But please allow me to finish so that you can understand the true depth of what is to come."

Eli nodded, so Cheung continued. "After I had regained my strength I learned the Zhe had fled with his prizes to the mountains of southern Yunnan Province. He then sold one of them on the black market to a wealthy European collector and used the money to finance a rather extravagant lifestyle in the Middle East. That figure finally came into my possession some years ago, but the other was sold to a powerful warlord named Old Tiger. That one we must get back at all costs – it's a matter of national honor and it was the last request of my dead friend."

The story sounded just as implausible to Eli as any he'd ever heard. But since he had no way to independently verify any part of it there was no choice but to accept it – but with caution. "So Mr. Cheung, you plan to pay me an enormous sum of money if I deliver the second statue back to you. I am also supposed to believe that it really should be returned to *you* and not the government here or in Taipei? And this is everything?"

Cheung angered rapidly, his face flushed red with emotion. "Mr. Ross, I do not intend to play these verbal games with you. It would be a waste of your time and mine. You have heard the *entire* story and I have to tell you that I initially felt no strong desire to share it with you. It was my niece who persuaded me to do it, and it now appears to have been a mistake on my part."

"Wait, hold on there," said Eli trying to calm him. "Put yourself in my shoes for a minute. How would you react to some wild tale about a statue and all that?"

"That is not my concern. So will you do the job or not?" He poured himself another cup of tea but quickly threw it to the ground in disgust. "Damn. Can't anyone understand what I mean when I say *hot*?"

"Your niece gave me a deposit of $10,000. If I take the job I want a total of $100,000 more, not including expenses. Fifty thousand guaranteed whether I bring it back or not. Take it or leave it."

Cheung stared at Eli with a vile and contemptuous look, trying to evaluate the seriousness of his proposal. "Mai Lee will accompany you on your travels. She will act as a facilitator since you speak no Mandarin, and will also be my representative. As such, she will have full authority to act with my name on any matters that are deemed appropriate by her. Will you agree to this?"

Eli felt like he was taking orders from Murray Morgenthal again, with his demand to 'protect his interests.' "Fine, whatever it takes to get things rolling."

"When you arrive in China you will meet with one of our men. He will provide you with the necessary travel documents and instructions as to where to find weapons and support in the area. You may go."

Eli stared past the old man and down at the foggy view of the harbor. The steel and glass towers jutted through the mist like sharp spikes ready to impale all passersby. Cheung swept past him into the house and clapped his hands sharply, barking orders to the servants while he walked. This looked to Eli to be the side of dear old "Uncle" that Mai Lee never got to see. The fog thickened rapidly and drifted in towards the house, bringing with it a damp chill that affected Eli more deeply than it should have. Soon it enveloped the veranda where he stood, and he was surrounded by the penetrating cloud. A shiver caught hold of him, so Eli grabbed the tea and poured another cup. It occurred to him that after all the time that had passed, he was right back in the fog again. Only it wasn't the air Eli was thinking of.

Chapter 6

"Did you have a nice chat with Uncle?" Mai Lee asked innocently as Eli escaped back into the living room.

"Yeah, everything went just great. I'd have to say that we have a unique understanding of one another now."

"Somehow I find it hard to believe that things went that smoothly," she said. "Uncle has a reputation for being a bit high-handed at times. He's even done so with me once or twice. And you're no angel, Lord knows." She smiled, and her eyes brightened Eli's mood.

The return trip on the *Star Ferry* was decidedly more relaxing than the first. Mai Lee was much more confident and reassured that the job would indeed begin as planned, and that everyone was on the same page. Eli was suspicious as usual, but survival had taught him to be that way when the situation was unclear; this one was as dark as tar. Wishing to change his frame of mind, he focused his attention on the girl. "You know, you're really very beautiful with your hair down, like this." He touched her smooth black mane and it dropped down around her shoulders like an obsidian waterfall.

She laughed, perhaps more from nervousness than amusement but stifled her outburst so as not to offend him. "Eli, really! Now don't go and dash all my preconceived notions about you by being nice."

"I wouldn't dream of it," Eli whispered, smiling softly. They were on their way to the first meeting Mai Lee had been able to set up, a discussion with an old business ally of Cheung's with some information to sell. It seemed strange to Eli that a business associate would sell an old friend information but that was the way things were in Hong Kong; if it couldn't be bought here, it didn't exist.

As the ferry bumped home against the dock the pair quickly made their way up the terminal to Salisbury Road. "Let's walk," she said, charging off down the busy street. Eli followed like a puppy after its mother and tried to keep up as she glided effortlessly through the teeming multitudes. It had turned unusually cool for a spring day in Hong Kong and the gentle breeze helped sweep away the claustrophobic feeling that kept clawing at him.

Eli was continually amazed by the compact nature of the city. The narrow streets were jammed with people; the massive traffic snarls and tiny shops made the place seem like a giant ant farm. He half expected a set of enormous eyes to peer down at them through the fog. They turned at the Peninsula Hotel and waded off through the crowds into the bustle of Hankow Road. Dodging the preoccupied people with their brand new cell phones became a challenge, since they seemed to drift about mindlessly as if guided by signals from the instruments. "Where are you dragging me?" Eli shouted over the din of the traffic.

"Haiphong Road. This is a short cut."

A short cut? Where? It didn't actually matter, since Eli was going to be paid even if he didn't come up with the statue. Rows and rows of jewelry and curio shops were broken only by the common luggage shops or herbalists, with their displays of ugly, twisted Ginseng roots. They turned at the corner of Haiphong Road and skirted past a couple of large delivery trucks that had pulled up on the sidewalk.

"Here we are," she announced proudly. "Six-sixteen." Mai Lee started up the dingy stairwell beside the grocery and rang the entry bell at the top of a small wrought iron gate. Eli carefully stepped over the fallen cabbage and lettuce leaves that carpeted the lower stairs and followed her in. The clean white door was labeled, "Wong Family Fine Custom Jewelry," stenciled poorly in red paint. Eli and Mai Lee entered the cramped, musty room, poorly lit by a pair of dim fluorescent lights and a jeweler's lamp. Mai Lee called out, "Mr. Wong? Hello, it's Mai Lee Jones."

"Yes, yes. Just a minute!" Some muffled banging of crockery from the back of the shop was the only other sign of life in the place. "Welcome my dear," said Wong as he appeared from behind a beaded curtain. He balanced a tray of biscuits and tea in his brown, liver-spotted hands which he extended very carefully. "It is very good to see you again my child. How is your illustrious uncle?" He embraced her furtively and offered a chair.

"Uncle is quite well, thank you. And you are well? Please, permit me to introduce Mr. Rose, my associate. He has just recently joined our staff."

"Good to meet you sir," said Eli, offering his hand. The old man waved it off and asked Eli to sit down.

"The pleasure is mine young man." He stroked his long white beard and poured three cups of boiling tea from his mended ceramic pot. "Do you know what this is, young guest?"

"Ginseng, if my nose serves me," Eli said, remembering the ugly roots from the herbalist's store front.

"My dear, this *gwailo* has a trace of culture. He's not like the others in your uncle's employ." The old man grinned. Mai Lee smiled and sipped her tea, a bit embarrassed. Wong continued to verbally poke his new visitor, knowing Eli was at his social mercy. "Do you know why we drink tea made from the Ginseng root, Mr. Rose?"

"No," Eli answered flatly, just wishing to end the small talk quickly.

"Because it brings us health and virility. It makes us

strong and replenishes our vitality." He gulped down a mouthful of the boiling liquid and poured another cup. Eli surmised that judging from Wong's appearance it hadn't worked very well. "Don't be deceived by your surroundings my young friend," he said, observing Eli inspecting his shop. "Even though I wear old clothes and have a long, white beard I am still very healthy. Why I could even sire a child if given half the chance," he laughed. "Such a pity I cannot find a nice girl to allow me the opportunity."

The old man smiled broadly. "Do you know I will be 84 years young next week? On that day, I will enjoy a fine meal at the home of my great-grand daughter and later I will try to find a beautiful woman with whom I can make passionate love." He howled at his comment and Mai Lee giggled and blushed with embarrassment.

Eli pretended to laugh a bit to be polite and said, "You don't have to convince me of your vitality sir. I'm learning fairly quickly that everything here is not exactly what it seems."

"Very good," he sighed. "So in spite of these humble surroundings I am a very wealthy and successful man."

"Mr. Wong," interrupted Mai Lee, finally becoming impatient, "you know why we are here. What can you tell us about a warlord named Old Tiger and do you know where we can find him?"

"Such impatience!" said the old man. The crude overhead lights reflected off his hairless scalp and lent an other-worldly glow to his demeanor. Wong stroked his snow-white beard and said, "Very well then, if you wish to behave so impertinently. You want to know where to find Old Tiger? Let me tell you, this is not a man you truly wish to find."

"So that's what he calls himself?" Eli asked.

"Yes, and with good reason. You see, Old Tiger has established himself as a warlord, something many people did not believe was still possible in these days. As I know the story, Old Tiger found refuge near the border areas of Vietnam, Burma, and the People's Republic after the Red Guard had pursued him from Guangzhou. He raised enough money through various "means" to pay and equip his own small army and now he lives in the jungle in high style. The Communists tried on three occasions to remove him and each time suffered humiliating losses without success. Old Tiger even fought on the side of Vietnam during the late 1979 border war with China. Imagine, fighting against one's own homeland in that way! But the Vietnamese had promised him asylum and a steady supply of men and guns for his cooperation, so this was too tempting for the old devil to refuse."

Wong shook his head and sipped his foul brew with gusto. "Now he is reviled in his homeland as a traitor. He is a jackal and dope smuggler who pollutes the world with his vile drugs, and even Vietnam has questioned the value of his presence. But this snake is very strong in the highlands and they cannot dislodge him easily."

"What kind of help and guidance can you give us, old friend?" Mai Lee asked somberly.

"Your uncle did not tell me the purpose of your visit, so I hesitate to say. I do not wish to have your fate on my conscience."

"I think you may be overly concerned, Mr. Wong," said Eli. "I have no intention of becoming anyone's martyr."

"It wasn't you I was thinking of," the old man said flatly and with a slight smirk. "Ah well, I suppose youth does give one a certain sense of immortality." He smiled and shook his head slowly. "I will tell you who to see in China. I will make the arrangements for your transportation but you must leave tomorrow."

"Thank you very much, sir," said Mai Lee reverently. She stood up to leave, prompting Eli to scramble quickly to his feet. "Uncle will be most generous with your compensation."

"Yes my dear, I know," he said from his chair. "I wish you good fortune and look forward to your safe return."

"Thank you for your help sir," said Eli. Before he could leave, Wong grabbed him tightly by the forearm and pulled him down close. His strength surprised Eli; *must be the Ginseng*, he thought.

"I am an old man, but that misfortune allows me to speak my mind without concern. I think you are a fool to do this, and you will only come to grief and misery because of it. You must stay aware of your surroundings, as there are some that will try and stop you." He paused for a second and then whispered, "But if you do succeed in finding Old Tiger I would like you to do something for me that I would pay much money to see."

"And what would that be?" Eli asked, anxious to leave.

"Please, kill him……….. slowly."

§

Eli and Mai Lee walked back to Beijing Road and climbed the stairs to the Crystal Jade Restaurant, searching for lunch and a place to talk over their next move. Eli asked for a table at the back of the room so he could watch the place without appearing to watch it.

Young girls pushed the stainless steel *dim sum* carts between the crowded tables and smiled at the diners as they proffered their wares. Eli allowed Mai Lee to order enough for both of them, deciding instead to focus his attention on the disposition of the exits. "You haven't said two words since we left Wong's," Mai Lee said quizzically. She poured two cups of steaming green tea and pulled a dumpling from one of the small bamboo steamers.

"I haven't said much? Well I guess that's because I've been trying to come up with the right words to express just how I feel about this whole mess. Somehow I've been left speechless by the whole thing." Eli sipped his tea slowly.

"Well you must have *something* to say?"

He sampled a spring roll and stared quietly at the animated diners scattered around the room. The whole plan really smelled from top to bottom, and Eli's sixth sense was nagging at him, telling him to run for the hills while he still could. "I'm just concerned, that's all. I mean, how do we know we can trust the old man to do what he says? How do we know he won't just sell us out to the Communists as a couple of spies or smugglers?"

"If Uncle says we can trust him then we can trust him," she stated curtly. "Uncle is very well connected outside of China but he goes to Mr. Wong whenever he needs to do business inside China. Mr. Wong has been very reliable, and is widely known and respected in certain circles as a patriot and hero."

Eli dropped 50 Hong Kong dollars on the table and waved at the waiter to take the change. "Let's walk," he said, pulling the girl after him. They wandered down past the shops in the general direction of the ferry, not speaking at first but then making small talk about nonsense like the price and authenticity of the pearls in the store windows. A greasy little guy in a vinyl bomber jacket jumped in front of Eli and shoved an arm full of watches in his face.

"Watch mister? Have good deal on Rolex. You want Rolex, mister?"

"What do you think?" Eli asked Mai Lee.

"I don't think so," she smiled, tugging at Eli's arm.

"Good deal, mister. Because you are my good friend only $20 U.S." The young guy seemed almost agitated by Eli's refusal to consider the purchase.

"Sorry, *amigo*. There's no such thing as a *bad* deal in this place." Eli walked away and joined Mai Lee at the corner. Unfortunately, he failed to notice that the guy had lowered his arm and waved towards the intersection. "Everyone has something to sell here don't they?"

"Yes," she sighed. "But that is the nature of Hong Kong. It's also the nature of the Chinese people. We are the traders of the world and the world has always attempted to get something from us for nothing. Perhaps that's what makes us attach a price tag to everything."

Emerging at the intersection with Canton Road Eli suddenly stopped and cupped her beautiful face in his hands. "Why is it that my instinct tells me to run away as fast as I can but I just can't seem to leave?"

"I don't know," she whispered, looking straight up into his eyes. "Perhaps there is something more in it for you than just money." Surprisingly, she kissed his hand lightly and quickly, then broke his embrace and walked towards the crosswalk. Her response caught Eli off guard and he overlooked a large delivery van parked unusually close to the corner on the other side of the road. His eyes rapidly refocused on the surroundings as a large red warning sign exploded in his brain: *that's the only van parked anywhere on this road*; *there is no driver in the cab*; *the van has no license plates*; *where's the greasy watch guy*? The scene ahead appeared to be a minor traffic violation, but Eli suddenly realized that was how it was meant to look.

"Mai Lee, wait a minute. Don't go out into the

street!" Eli yelled, but not fast enough. As he ran down the sidewalk a hooded figure jumped from the rear of the van and leveled a Mini-Uzi submachine gun at the girl's lovely chest. She turned as Eli called out and didn't see the assassin's approach. The whole thing played out in slow motion and Eli felt like his feet were cast in cement. "Move!" Eli screamed. "Move, move, move!" She whirled around to see the gunman rushing at her from 10 feet away. The guy pulled back the bolt on the gun as the crowd on the sidewalk shouted and scattered in all directions. Eli's mind was in overdrive as he got to the corner. An eternity seemed to pass as the guy stopped in the middle of the crosswalk and squared himself to shoot. Eli watched helplessly as he pulled the trigger, and he waited for the awful sound he knew would soon follow.

Chapter 7

Good *joss*, she told Eli later. Hong Kong Chinese frequently use the word to describe the God of Fate, and the gods were definitely smiling on them that day. Life sometimes takes those kinds of turns, and it just as well could have turned out very differently. But on that particular afternoon Eli was as lucky as he'd ever been.

The gun jammed! The assassin stood there in the middle of the crosswalk dumbfounded. On one of the busiest streets in all of Hong Kong the guy stood in full view of at least 2000 people, jerking and hammering frantically on the bolt, vainly squeezing the trigger. Eli shoved Mai Lee to the ground like a wet rag as he dashed past her and out into the street. He blasted into the thug at full speed and they both toppled backwards into the gutter while the gun flew past them onto the sidewalk. The Uzi hit the concrete violently and went off, sending several shots in the direction of the amazed crowd of onlookers. The loud reports momentarily shocked Eli back to his senses and he reached out to grab the weapon. The assassin jumped to his feet and tackled Eli just short of the gun. The guy was surprisingly tough for his size and he used his fleeting advantage to reach behind his head for a long thin-blade knife which he then tried to jam in Eli's neck. Eli moved sideways and the assassin shoved the blade into the asphalt, breaking it at the hilt. Eli flipped his elbow up into the guy's nose and the assassin shrieked as he flew backwards onto the street.

Eli sprang to his feet and pulled the guy up by his shirt, throwing him head first into the side of the van. The sound of police sirens caused Eli to wheel around and look down the road. At that moment a large black Mercedes suddenly burst through the crowd on the sidewalk and skidded to a stop next to the van. Two guys jumped out of the car and dragged their stunned comrade from the street, tossing him into the back seat. The car shot off down the small side street and was gone from view in a second.

"Quickly!" gasped Mai Lee. "We must not be here when the police arrive." She grabbed Eli's arm and they ran through the chattering crowd down the street. Eli recovered quickly as they sped down to the ferry landing just in time to catch the 5 o'clock back to Hong Kong.

Eli paused to adjust his tie and Mai Lee gripped the white railing tightly as the lethargic old boat motored towards the setting sun. "Damn it!" Eli cursed loudly, attracting curious stares from the passengers seated nearby. He smacked the rail hard with his open hand and shook his head in anger. "I must be getting old. How could I have been so stupid?"

"Eli, don't be so hard on yourself," gasped Mai Lee as she tried to catch her breath. "I think you were fantastic." She squeezed his hand hard. "It's just not possible for you to be everywhere at once."

"Look - that's what you're paying me for, and I screwed it up. We were just damn lucky today, unbelievably lucky. One more second and that guy would have had the bolt free. We would have been a blip on the evening news."

"But it didn't happen that way," she said calmly.

Mai Lee stared deeply into Eli's eyes as the light evening breeze filtered softly through her smooth hair. She made it seem as though nothing unusual had happened all day. The afterglow of the setting sun warmed her brown features so that her skin glowed like a fresh peach. Her gaze made Eli's stomach tense and he felt that their business "relationship" might be headed in the wrong direction. *Not now*, he thought. He would consider things differently after the job was over.

"Look, I appreciate your consideration but I screwed up, plain and simple. It won't happen again, I promise." The girl stood there staring at him silently, holding his hand tightly. Eli hugged her for a second and then made her sit down on one of the seats near the railing. "Mai Lee," said Eli, "let's try to concentrate on something else for a minute. Who wants you so badly?

The obvious choice is that Old Tiger has somehow got wind of your mission, but how would he know we were on to him so soon?"

She shook her head slowly. "I don't really know. But it's obvious we have a problem. I knew it was true even at the Ocotal. I'm sorry I ever listened to Uncle and dragged you into this."

"Forget about that. I wouldn't have come if I hadn't been interested. It's not your fault."

She smiled and looked up at him with her large, deep eyes. Eli felt the sudden urge to kiss her, but was able to restrain himself. "Eli, I think I need to talk to you about something."

"Stop," Eli ordered. "Hold on. Let's just solve one problem at a time, Ok? What's the next move on our vacation?"

She sighed and said, "Tomorrow morning we go to Kai Tak and fly to Guangzhou. Uncle and Mr. Wong will have arranged for a member of the resistance to contact us, and this person will help us to locate Old Tiger." The bumping of the ferry signaled their arrival and they walked out to find Baizhu waiting with the car for the return to the Peak House.

Mai Lee collapsed into the large back seat and reached for the brandy bottle in the mini-bar. She poured a large glass for herself and offered one to Eli but he declined, trying to stay focused on the myriad of problems that they had. "You know Eli, it's been a very long time since I've felt the kinds of things for someone that I'm feeling right now for you." She cuddled next to him and drained her glass as the car started up Victoria

Peak. The sharp curves of the narrow street caused Mai Lee to press her own smooth curves against him seductively, and Eli's thoughts began to drift again. "Eli, are you listening to me?" She poured another glass and quickly tossed down the contents.

"Sorry. I'm just trying to sort a few things out."

"Well, try not to think too much about it now. Tomorrow is a new day, and we'll be much closer to finishing this thing." She took Eli's hand softly again, but this time brought it through the slit in her dress and between her incredibly smooth legs. Her heat seared his brain and she added, "Besides, it's still early and very warm." Burning was a better word to describe how Eli felt, but he forced himself not to be drawn in any closer. She rubbed his hand against herself, uttering a low and seductive gasp, all the while breathing warm and quick breaths against his neck. "Eli........Eli, you're not paying attention."

Eli's reaction told him he was, but he tried to brush off the comment. "Sure I am, boss. But there won't be any saluting tonight. Time to go."

§

She pouted all the way to the airport and the hangover didn't improve her mood, either. Eli shook his head at the thought of how he was able to resist Mai Lee's substantial charms. But after all, this was supposed to be business. They bumped and jostled their way through Security and Immigration and soon queued up with their fellow travelers at the China

Airlines gate. Most of their traveling companions appeared to be asleep or were nearly so, and didn't seem at all apprehensive about the trip. Eli had often heard the play off of CAAC's acronym - "China Airlines Almost Crashes" - but never thought much about it until then. "You know what we call this airline?" said Mai Lee with a giggle.

"Yes," Eli replied. "So you're not still mad at me about last night?"

"No, not really. But if there ever is a next time, I will expect a certain degree of cooperation or I'll wonder whether you like me or not."

"Don't worry," Eli laughed. "When we get back to Hong Kong I'll cooperate all you like." She laughed as they boarded the ancient turboprop, a 25-year old Russian Antonov AN-24D. Recognition of the plane's make and reputation made the hair on the back of Eli's neck stand up. They squeezed into their cramped, dirty seats and strapped in for the flight. The old plane creaked and popped as it sauntered down the runway but it managed to lift smoothly off the ground. The cabin quickly filled with cigarette smoke and they were on their way.

"A friend will be at the airport to meet us," said Mai Lee quietly. "First, we will check in at the White Swan Hotel and then find Mr. Wong's local contact. He will tell us how to locate our prize."

Eli nodded but didn't speak. His visa was approved for only eight days and one entry so they had no choice but to finish the job in one try. The stewardess interrupted their quiet briefing with a customary gift from the airline - a set of plastic aviation wings with the CAAC logo at the center. The gift of plastic seemed an appropriate metaphor for their venture. "*Xie xie*," Eli said in thanks, and the androgynous stewardess smiled back and bowed slightly. The plane touched down hard after the one hour flight and Eli was relieved to see that the terminal was covered and, possibly, air conditioned. The old jet taxied to a stop and they joined the rest of the passengers aboard a solidly packed bus for the 50 yard ride to the dingy terminal. The building was in the process of some kind of renovation, though it was difficult to tell whether the current state was demolition or reconstruction.

"You see there - that is the Immigration and Customs line," said Eli's beautiful guide. Mai Lee maneuvered them to the front of the line so that they could clear the confusion quickly. On her advice the pair had dressed casually and carried their small bags on the plane to avoid the frenzy of baggage claim. Eli watched as their fellow travelers stood by, their things dumped in an unsorted pile before them. They were left to scramble through the pile for their belongings, unassisted by the disinterested ground crew. The nearby free-for-all caused enough of a diversion with the Customs officials that they quickly waved the pair through without checking their duffels. A large crowd of waiting relatives and friends jostled and elbowed each other just beyond the Customs area, trying to get a glimpse of the ever growing pile of people and bags in the baggage area. Eli and Mai Lee pushed through and were suddenly grabbed by a small man holding a cardboard sign that read, "Hunt."

Mai Lee greeted him in Cantonese and then introduced Eli using his real name. "Please meet you," smiled the toothless little guy. His name was Deng, like the current Party Chairman, and he seemed as soft-spoken as his diminutive frame would suggest. He insisted upon carrying the bags, which he unceremoniously tossed into the back of his red mini-van. Once inside Mai Lee sighed noticeably, finally free of the turmoil of the visitor's area. The engine of the tiny vehicle coughed and jolted to life and they zipped off down the bumpy, tree-lined drive that led to the city. The road was somewhat reminiscent of the entrance to the Beijing airport, and Eli reflected on the fact that the trees must have been mandated by "The Party" for every airport drive. Mai Lee and Deng chatted in Cantonese and Eli quickly realized that his 10 words of Mandarin would be nearly useless in the southern provinces.

Eli gathered from Mai Lee's reaction that problems had already developed with their plans. "Mr. Deng tells me that our main contact man was a salesman in the local market. He was arrested last night by the city police for some type of petty crime - he shoplifted a pair of Levi's or something like that, I'm not quite certain."

"So when will he be able to meet us?" Eli asked

naively.

"He won't be able to meet us," Mai Lee answered glumly. "It seems this was his third offense and he will be sent to a regional prison near Wuhan for "re-education and training." We'll have to go to Qing Ping Market ourselves to get our travel papers. They were probably hidden in with his personal effects. Fortunately, Mr. Deng has kindly agreed to assist us." He nodded as if on cue and smiled his empty-toothed smile into the rear-view mirror. Eli smiled back in acknowledgement.

The city closed in rapidly around the little van, as if it was being swallowed by a huge, antiquated whale. The tiny vehicle was quickly enveloped in the grayness of the place, jammed into the narrow streets lined with their dirty, crumbling buildings. Guangzhou reminded Eli of a run-down version of Hong Kong, one that looked as if it had been bombed first and then partially rebuilt. Nevertheless, that same vibrant pace permeated the streets, a cacophony of motion going in all directions at once. The place overflowed with humanity. At times people practically appeared to be bursting forth from the shops and small restaurants, spilling into the bicycle paths that bordered the highway on both sides. Their dominant mode of travel was still the bicycle, a vehicle the Chinese had poured out into the developing world with great success. They were simple examples of the machine, without the frills and supposed necessities western manufacturers feel are mandatory for their more elaborate versions. With names like "Flying Pigeon" and "Swift Fawn" they massed and flowed in great flocks beside the van.

The pressing conformity of communism was still apparent everywhere, from the depressing 1950's Soviet-style office buildings to the frothing, white-shirted masses. However, every so often a brightly colored shirt or dress would glide by, meek exclamations to the principle of individuality that was still so frowned-upon by their iron-fisted leaders. But change was everywhere inside the rotting totalitarian shell that was once as solid as the Great Wall, and Eli knew one day it would eventually burst out. From the Pearl River Bridge Eli could see a large, multi-level hotel with a large swan on its side, the well-known White Swan. "I see a piece of the 20th century ahead," he exclaimed sarcastically.

Mai Lee noted his tone and stated, "You know, Guangzhou is much better off than most cities in China. The economy here is very open to the west and much more adapted to capitalism than even Beijing. These joint venture hotels are just the most visible benefits but there are others." Eli sat quietly, staring at the deteriorating *façades* of the old European-style buildings of the embassy district that bordered the hotel. Mai Lee fired off a few more instructions to Deng who nodded respectfully. He pulled the van through the circular front driveway and stopped in front of one of the huge stone lions that guarded the hotel's front entrance. Mai Lee called out orders to the sharply attired bellboys and a path was cleared through the tourists that filled the lobby so they could pass without delay.

The gaping lobby captivated locals and tourists alike. A clear symbol intended as a portent of better times to come, the place was the size of a small amusement park, Eli thought. A huge Chinese sampan carved from a single block of jade rose up from the middle of the floor and served as a suitable backdrop for people to pose for photos. For those that found faux-natural wonders more to their tastes, a 15-foot high waterfall in the back of the lobby emptied into a small lagoon filled with enormous *coy* fish. All this was surrounded by life-sized pear trees also made of jade.

"This is quite a place, isn't it?" said Mai Lee.

"Sure is," he replied. "But I've got to say I'm more than a little surprised at how ostentatious it is. I thought things like these have been taboo since the days of Pu Yi."

"China is not the same place that it was 10 years ago or even five years ago for that matter. A new revolution is taking place here - an economic one. Even the government bureaucrats realize they have to continue to attract foreign investment to the country and joint ventures like this one, no matter how unthinkable in the past, are encouraged now."

"Wow, great propaganda for "The Party," Eli joked.

"I don't mean to sound that way but I am hopeful that the reforms that permitted what you see here will carry on and be extended to other areas. This place is one of the symbols of hope for me, the hope that after the handover, Beijing will let Hong Kong continue to be Hong Kong. I suppose we'll just have to see how it goes." Mai Lee smiled wistfully and turned to fill out the registration documents. They dashed up to the room and unpacked, changed clothes and headed back down to the lobby to meet Deng. He was sitting by the waterfall with his spindly little legs crossed, leisurely smoking a cigarette. The little guy jumped to his feet when he caught sight of Mai Lee and squashed the cigarette frantically onto the freshly waxed floor. "He's upset because I asked him not to smoke around me," said Mai Lee casually as they approached. Deng bowed slightly and Eli smiled and did the same. Mai Lee shot out a rapid flow of Cantonese and Deng turned to leave. "Ok, let's go," she added. The trio walked out the front entrance and into the waiting mini-van.

Chapter 8

Deng piloted the sputtering vehicle back through the old embassy area towards the Qing Ping Market for their expected rendezvous with the travel papers. "Have you ever been to a typical outdoor Chinese market?" asked Mai Lee innocently as they neared the entrance.

"No, not a real one."

"Well perhaps you should know a few things before we go in. Most westerners are usually a bit unprepared the first time. You see there is a saying that roughly means that the southern Chinese will eat anything that has fins, wings, arms, or legs, except a chair. This might seem amusing but coupled with the belief that all ingredients in Chinese cooking must be as fresh as possible, some pretty gruesome and inhumane things can be seen in these markets. At least, that's what the *gwailos* say."

"And what do you say?"

"I see both viewpoints. My people say that food is food and nothing more. Because I was educated in England I have seen how people in the west treat their animals, at least those you might think of as pets. I suppose there is value in that practice but I think something like that is more common when you have an abundance of food to go around." She pointed at the crumbling apartments that lined the road near the market entrance and added, "There have been times when we have not been so fortunate. Old habits die hard. In any case you'll need a strong stomach"

Deng squeezed the small van onto the cracked sidewalk and they disembarked and waded into the bustling crowd. Deng slipped smoothly through the frenetic mass of shoppers with Mai Lee close behind. Eli struggled to keep up without blundering through the narrow pathways like a bull. Vendors shouted their specialties at the passersby with agitated vigor, who were equally vocal in turn, especially when a price was to be negotiated.

Exotic smells mingled in the damp air with wisps of cigarette smoke and the stench of death. Eli concentrated on being especially careful not to knock over the merchandise, like the sacks of ugly Ginseng roots or dried insects that jammed the herbalist's stalls. "Mai Lee, what do they use the dried bees for?"

"Medicine," she shouted over her shoulder. Deng had stopped just ahead at the end of the dried good's area, and waved in broad sweeps for Eli and Mai Lee to follow quickly. The more open part of the market featured a collection of familiar and odd vegetables and an equally familiar and odd assortment of wildlife. Kittens shared exhibition space with soft-shelled turtles, fresh water eels, black-skinned chickens, and owls. Mai Lee must have noticed the expression of surprise on Eli's face because she walked back and said, "I warned you you'd need a strong stomach."

Eli nodded his head, but couldn't restrain his westerner's judgment of the locals treatment of animals. Deng had found the now empty stall of their former contact man. He was a salted eel vendor from Sanya and had been engaged to transfer the critical documents because he was the cousin of Mai Lee's third cousin. Mai Lee and Deng quickly pulled the guy in the neighboring stall into an animated conversation so Eli used his lack of involvement as an opportunity to scan the place for emergency exits. Any rapid movements through that crowd seemed like a ludicrous idea so the main exits were out of the question. Fortunately, there was a possible exit right next to them where one of the turtle salesmen had stacked his empty crates up to the top of the retaining wall. Eli scanned the crowd for anything out of the ordinary; the overly curious local, a shopper that may have been overdressed for a stop at the market, but saw nothing. In his previous visit to China he noted that the average curious citizen usually broke off his stare when you made eye contact, somewhat like the way a cat appears uncomfortable with a similar response. Eli's attention wandered through the crowd from one pair of curious eyes to another and each person's gaze was quickly averted when he stared back...........with the exception of one guy in particular.

Mai Lee and Deng had meanwhile convinced the turtle man to surrender their ex-contact's personal gear, which he'd held for "safe keeping" until the guy returned to claim them. Too bad that the guy would likely never need them again. Mai Lee rapidly rifled through the odd bits of clothing and toiletries until she turned up a large manila envelope. "Got it!" she exclaimed, holding it out to Eli. Just as he was about to take it from her a hand shot in like lightning and ripped the envelope away. Eli yelled at the guy as he started to run and the shock of his voice caused the guy to look back momentarily, a fatal mistake on his part. The instant he looked back at Eli he collided violently with two guys carrying a large sack of green onions.

Eli seized the opportunity and fell on the skinny guy as hard as he could, ramming his forearm into the guy's neck. The thief's head smacked hard into the greasy pavement. It sounded like someone had dropped a cantaloupe onto the concrete from a second story window. The guy groaned and sagged limply like a soup noodle, so Eli tore the envelope from his hand and thrust it back at Mai Lee. "Would you please be a little more careful next time," Eli said, jerking the kid to his feet with a shake.

Mai Lee shouted a few Cantonese phrases at the young guy, who stood there mutely bleeding from the wound on his head. He tried to ignore her by looking away into the crowd. "Hang on a second," said Eli, and then stomped down hard on the kid's ragged tennis shoe. He let out a yelp and Eli grabbed him stiffly by the collar and shoved him toward Mai Lee. Deng looked around like a spooked deer while Mai Lee questioned him again more forcefully. A crowd was gathering and jabbering away, pointing and staring at the commotion. Things like this rarely ever happened at Qing Ping Market, even on the most unusual of days. The skinny thug finally exploded with a torrent of Cantonese that came so quickly it even surprised Mai Lee. Deng interrupted unexpectedly and said something to her, then walked off towards the mini-van.

The grimy little weasel continued his dialog with Mai Lee for a few more seconds until he seemed to stop suddenly in mid syllable. Eli looked at him and the guy's eyes were wide open but staring blankly. *I've seen this reaction before,* he thought. Just as he began to search his dim memory Eli noticed that he suddenly had to support the guy's entire weight. Eli checked behind the guy, fearing what he'd find. Sure enough, a small red spot had appeared just below the thief's left shoulder blade and it began to grow larger by the second. "Damn it!" shouted Eli, but before he could react a second bullet impacted into the back of the guy's head, splattering some people just behind them with blood, bone and brains. "Move!" Eli screamed at Mai Lee, dropping the guy in a crumpled heap on the market floor. He yanked her by the arm towards the pile of crates he'd seen earlier and she got the message quickly. The dead crook caused no immediate reaction from the crowd since he appeared to be sleeping, but that quickly changed when the contents of his skull began to flow out onto the concrete.

Mai Lee had reached the top of the crates when the screaming and shouting started in the crowd. Eli could see two well-dressed guys running towards them from the far entrance and reasoned that they weren't coming to offer help. The girl hopped over the wall and Eli jumped onto the crates and followed her in one motion. "This way!" she shouted and they dashed down to the corner and out of the market. As they ran she gasped, "What did you do to him?"

"Me? I didn't do anything - somebody else got to him first." They stopped and looked for the two hit men. "How do we get out of this fucking place?"

"Follow," she panted and ran off in the direction of the hotel. The shouting rapidly faded into the normal background noise of the city as they trotted, then walked into the old embassy area. "Now we're really in it," added Mai Lee after a few moments.

"You're telling me! Did you get anything out of him?"

"Not much. He was rambling - I could hardly follow him. At first he said he thought there might be some money in the packet but after you "persuaded" him to be more honest he said that someone had paid him to harass us and keep us there."

"That's it?" Eli asked in disappointment.

"Well there was one other thing. Did you notice the

tattoo on his hand - two hands clasped below a skull? That's the sign of Old Tiger." Mai Lee sat down on one of the stone benches that lined the walkway and tried to catch her breath. "It's sort of amusing when you think about it," she added with a sigh. "The old bastard has a flair for the dramatic but I am really starting to get tired of this."

Eli sat down beside her and smacked his hand on the bench in disbelief. "*Now* you're starting to get tired of this? Two attempts on your life didn't bother you, eh?"

"I guess I thought we might be able to move around in China like couple of tourists. I should have known that would be impossible with a *gwailo*. And there are so many eyes in Hong Kong. I see now that I was naive to believe our trip could be kept quiet." Mai Lee sighed again and looked deeply into his eyes. "Really, I didn't know it was going to be like *this*." They sat there staring at each other for a few long seconds and then she said, "If you want to pull out I'll certainly understand why. It's too dangerous to continue now since even the local authorities are probably trying to find us."

"No chance," said Eli, pulling the her close. "We'll manage but we've got to lose Old Tiger's people before we can continue this mess." Eli paused for a moment and realized that they had done exactly what they needed to do. "How well do you trust Wong's network? I mean, do you think it was Deng that tipped the bad guys?"

Mai Lee shook her head and stared down at the

brick walkway. "I don't think so. He's harmless. Everything just checked out so well, even through our own sources here. I don't see how we could have missed something so obvious."

"Ok then," said Eli. "As we sit here we have all the freedom of movement we could ever want. I respectfully suggest we look at the travel papers, make our plans, and get the hell out of here.......boss."

Mai Lee opened the envelope and pulled out two CAAC airline tickets and a small map with some Chinese characters written on it. "The tickets are one way from Guangzhou to Haikou. The note on the map says to go to the Dadong Hai Hotel in Sanya. We have to meet a contact in the town tomorrow morning at 10:45. There's really not much more."

"Then it's time to pack," Eli said smiling. "When do we leave?"

"This afternoon. I've got to find Mr. Deng and tell him to............"

"To what? Let's just let Mr. Deng sleep quietly wherever he is without having to worry about us," Eli shot back quickly. "Humor me just this once, Ok?"

The girl smiled and said, "If you say so. Let's get back to the hotel and get our things."

"Sorry, but your trusted employee here doesn't advise that either."

She looked at Eli with a combination of curiosity and frustration. "Well perhaps I should just leave this whole thing to you then."

Eli lost his temper and grabbed her arm sharply,

moving close to her perfect lips to speak. "Look boss lady, it's time to start acting your IQ and not your shoe size. We have to stop making it so damn easy for every dickhead in the world to find us. Got it?"

She tried to pull her arm away but Eli held on and twisted it a bit. Mai Lee winced for a moment and spat back, "Alright then, I've got it. You're the expert – so what do you want to do?"

He pushed her reddened arm back and took firm hold of her shoulders. "We use our brains for a change. First we visit a store so we can buy some clean clothes, something less western. They'll be watching all the big hotels including ours, so we can kiss our stuff good-bye. Then we find a cheap local place and stay indoors until we're ready to go to the airport. Even though they'll be watching for us they don't know where we're going or when. My guess is we'll be able to pass through with the mass of humanity as a cover if we're really lucky. Ok?"

She looked back at Eli defiantly for a second and then her expression changed. Her eyes filled with tears and she buried her head in his chest. "I'm sorry," she sobbed. "I've been so bloody stupid about this. I let my pride get in the way and I've gone and mucked the whole thing up. I almost got us killed but probably got at least two other men killed, everyone is looking for us, I........"

Eli shook the girl back to attention, interrupting her emotional confession in mid-stream. "Mai Lee, you have to focus! We don't have time for this. Forget about them. They knew the risks just like us and their luck just ran out. We've got to keep that from happening to us and feeling sorry for ourselves is not going to get us anywhere but dead. Now let's get on with it." Mai Lee nodded and brushed her tears away. "Stay here," she said. I'll stand a better chance of getting one of the hotel taxis without you."

She walked down the street to the front of the hotel where Eli was able to watch her flag down a taxi without having to go to the entrance. *Thank God*, he thought. *So far, so good.* The taxi sped back and Eli jumped in the back seat while the car was still moving. Mai Lee was able to determine after a brief conversation that a nearby Friendship Store would probably be the best bet for acceptable clothing.

The driver deposited them at the entrance to the store and the couple moved quickly through the place, grabbing just enough of the necessities to last a few days. Eli found a good suitcase for their reservoir of clean clothes and then they were off to find a hotel. The driver pointed out some places to Mai Lee that she didn't even want to consider, based on their well-worn exteriors or the surrounding neighborhoods. They pulled up in front of the Guangzhou Hotel, a place that catered more to the overseas Chinese tourists than to westerners and Mai Lee said, "Wait here while I check this place out." Eli sat in the back seat exchanging occasional stiff smiles with the driver until she ran back out and up to the car. "This will do."

The new suitcase was pulled from the trunk and Eli gave the driver 30 FEC for his trouble. "*Xie, xie,*" he smiled and drove off. Mai Lee hurriedly but calmly checked them in and they took the decrepit old elevator to the third floor. The dim hall lights worked well enough to just disguise the filthy carpets and soiled walls, but the stench of mold and cigarette smoke was nearly overpowering and permeated everything. Mai Lee threw herself onto the bed and kicked her shoes off. "My feet are killing me," she said rubbing them gingerly. "By the way I did manage by dumb luck to have maps for several Chinese cities in my bag when we left the White Swan so I can show you where I think we need to go."

Eli reached into her shoulder bag and pulled a plastic bag full of oddly folded maps from the bottom. "Look for the one that has an enlargement of Hainan Island," she said, grimacing as she rubbed her left foot. "There, that's the one. Let me see, where is the place? Ok, I've got it." She stopped rubbing momentarily to point at a small spot on the south coast of the island. "That's it, there - Sanya."

Eli held her foot and began to work out the soreness with deep, circular motions. Mai Lee groaned and said, "That's wonderful. Ok, you rub and I'll show you where we're going." She pointed to a large city on the north coast and added, "This is Haikou, the largest city on Hainan Island. We're supposed to fly in there and then make our way to Sanya, here. The map that was left for us seems to show where the meeting is supposed to take place."

"So how do we get to Sanya?" Eli said, twisting her ankle gently. "And any chance of finding those weapons your uncle mentioned?"

"I'm afraid we lost that information with Mr. Wong's contact." She closed her eyes for a second and moaned, "Oh, that's very good. As for the trip, we can take the bus the whole way." Eli moved to within a few inches of her full, moist lips and stared down at the map as she pointed out the route.

"So the "X" that marks the spot for the meet is in downtown Sanya?" he added, his hot breath on her cheek.

"Not exactly, but this map does have a red dot on one of the streets. We can ask directions once we reach the town."

"Think your uncle's contact will find us there?" Eli whispered moving closer.

The girl looked up at him languidly, only an inch from his expectant mouth and almost within reach. "I'm certain that once we get close, very close, he'll know just what he should do."

Chapter 9

Nothing. That's what they saw as they slipped along with the crowd at the airport. Nothing out of the ordinary and no one that looked suspicious. Eli was never sure whether such clean exits were due more to good fortune, good planning, or some combination thereof. Even the ubiquitous Deng was nowhere to be found. Eli was convinced he'd set them up, whether for money or something more precious and was determined to stay skeptical about all Mai Lee's "contacts" in the future. She still refused to believe that Deng had given them up to the "Bad Guys," whoever they were, and wouldn't even talk about the possibility even after several hours had passed.

The flight took nearly two hours during which Eli made himself useful examining every map the girl had brought with her. Based on what he could glean from the enclosed Sanya city map, the meeting was to occur on a side street just off the main drag. Eli liked the idea better than the previous meeting point since it looked like there were a number of potential escape routes available. He'd just have to wait until he saw the place before he could plan anything definite.

The flight landed in Haikou with the characteristic CAAC bounce, rolling to a stop near several Chinese MiG 21F-13's (J-7's) and J-8II's. Eli was amused to see them there, jammed together at the far end of the runway looking like angry horseflies. He guessed that the Chinese leaders had never anticipated that their new approach to economic liberalism and the subsequent influx of western tourists would eventually lead to the inspection of their air force by former intelligence operatives. Eli was certain that some general's head would probably roll if Beijing ever found out. In other days such information would have been a boon to his government friends, but now the planes were merely an interesting distraction. After witnessing the baggage debacle in Guangzhou, Eli reacted quickly to the routine in Haikou and grabbed their bag before the locusts descended. Mai Lee searched for someone to ask about the bus to Sanya, focusing on a People's Liberation Army guard as a likely information source. This unnerved the hell out of Eli but he reminded himself of how poorly information traveled through China. There was almost no chance the young soldier had heard anything about the fugitives.

Mai Lee got the information she wanted and said, "Over there," pointing towards a small bus station. She'd secured two tickets to Sanya before Eli knew what had happened and he was pleased to see her pride in the simple act. He wanted her to regain her self confidence; it was impossible for him to work effectively without her. Nevertheless, he still reserved the right to question everything at any time. "The man said we had to hurry because they are just about to leave." The driver's helper stowed their bag on the roof and they found seats in one of the middle rows, much to the enjoyment of the surrounding passengers. Eli couldn't tell if they were chattering because of him or because of the fact that he and Mai Lee were obviously traveling together. In either case they were jovial enough that the dauntingly long trip seemed at least endurable. The door slammed shut and the bus shuddered away from the station with a sudden lurch. The dusty, palm-lined streets reminded Eli a little of Playa Coco though the common work groups of soldiers were a definite change. "It appears that the government has a surplus of men these days," injected Mai Lee, who seemed to have been reading his mind.

"What else do they have to do?" Eli asked rhetorically. "No war, no revolution, no one to crush or subjugate. Must be kind of boring for them." Mai Lee only smiled and Eli turned his thoughts to what remained unfinished in their quest. The implication from each of these meetings had been that the statue lay at the proverbial end of road, but they were once again packing off to some other place. It occurred to him, and not for the first time that the whole thing might just be a wild goose chase. Eli was also a worried about Mai Lee's total faith in others to provide an avenue of escape should they need one, since Old Tiger obviously wouldn't part with his beloved possession willingly. He needed weapons or some means of protection before he would be comfortable trying to pull this off. Besides, getting away with the statue and living to tell about it was definitely high on his priority list. Perhaps the girl really didn't understand just how deeply they had sunk themselves even if Eli knew better. His excuse, he reasoned somewhat objectively, was that he needed the money and, clearly needed the adrenaline rush of the action. Vicente warned him that would happen and Eli now regretted not having listened to him more closely at the time.

Being led all over southern China was certainly not his idea of a proactively driven mission. Eli bounced along for hour after mindless hour shifting and sorting everything he could remember and deduce about the job, from the first conversation to the last five minutes. The only common denominator was that he was being led through most of it rather than doing the leading. Eli was determined to play a more forceful role in Sanya, regardless of the consequences. Despite the near misses in Hong Kong and Guangzhou the whole operation still seemed too smooth to him. Go here, go there, meet this guy, go someplace else. Maybe it really wasn't any more complicated than that but the situation still bothered him. He kept getting the feeling that the whole thing was being managed from afar, like they were puppets in a puppet show. But if something like that was true the puppet master would never expect one of his toys to act independently. If he was wrong, Eli would just look foolish which wasn't a new position for him by any means. But if he was right and he altered the predetermined flow of events just slightly, any hidden traps or bad guys should pop right out of the woodwork like knotholes.

Mai Lee dozed off and on as did most of their traveling companions. The bumping and jerking gradually worked like a giant pacifier, a sleep-inducer for the over-mature and immature alike. The passengers slept not in spite of the ride but because of it. Eli remembered seeing several large trucks pass them with their open, flat beds full of sleeping workmen. They were nearly comatose, to the point that only severe, life-threatening jolts would barely rouse them to semi-consciousness. Hours passed for the bus passengers in this way. The small settlements they passed resembled scattered Stone Age huts more than late 20th century homes, though at least one naked light bulb hung in each dwelling. Thomas Edison would have been proud. Even the black and white television had found its way to Hainan, and the rare working model usually had a crowd of spectators around it, much like Eli's former adopted home.

The bus and passengers were equally beaten by the end of the day-long journey. The Dadong Hai Hotel was therefore a welcome sight, especially after the driver agreed to drop Eli and Mai Lee at the entrance for only 10 extra *Yuan*. Mai Lee handled the customary registration duties, cooperating dutifully with the disinterested young desk clerk. The pair dragged themselves up the concrete stairwell to their second floor room.

"Heavens it's good to be off that bus," exclaimed the girl, collapsing onto the bed.

"You can say that again. So what's the next move?"

"Well first," she said, stretching languidly, "I move we get something to eat. Later on, a walk on the beach might be in order. Tomorrow at 10:15 we should be in beautiful Sanya. That's the agenda. Any questions?"

"Not one. Let's find what passes for the restaurant and get this over with."

She looked perplexed by Eli's comment and said, "But I thought you liked Chinese food?"

"I do," he answered, "but something tells me I'm about to receive an introduction to the more exotic side the cuisine has to offer."

"Never fear my dear," she grinned. "I'll take good care of you."

It wasn't long before Eli regretted Mai Lee's judgment once again. "What the hell are those things?" he exclaimed, pointing at the heaping plate of mystery meat. "Those aren't monkey hands are they? I've heard they eat monkeys around here and I absolutely refuse to eat a relative, no matter how distant."

The girl laughed heartily and crowed, "Lord no, those aren't hands. Haven't you ever seen chicken feet? I thought you were supposed to be an experienced and worldly traveler?"

"Where did you ever get that idea?" Eli grimaced. "That only applies to things I can recognize as part of some real plant or animal. What's the rest of the meal supposed to be?"

She laughed and swept her thick black hair from her shoulder with a wave. "Tonight we're having two local delicacies: sea snake soup and steamed sand worms with squid. The waiter said they were very fresh."

"How charming," Eli sneered, his stomach suddenly feeling full. He glanced out at the lobby and noticed the bar was unoccupied and calling to him subliminally. A beer seemed like a perfect complement to the meal so Eli suffered through the bony sea snakes and the rubbery, but tasty sand worms. "Ok boss, I'm off duty. It's Miller time."

"It's what?" she queried.

"Haven't you ever heard that before – it's *Miller* time? In the States it's what we say when it's time for a beer. Or at least we *used* to say that. I guess I don't really know what people say now."

"No, sorry," she sighed tiredly. "Never heard that before, but the idea is brilliant. How 'bout a walk on the beach afterwards?"

"It's a deal." They walked across the lobby and into the tiny bar and Eli asked the disinterested waitress for a liter bottle of Zhujiang beer and two glasses.

"You weren't kidding about the beer," said Mai Lee with raised eyebrows.

Eli poured and offered a toast. "Here's to a quick end to this mess and to fulfillment of both our goals.

Gan bei!" Mai Lee smiled at his stilted use of the Mandarin phrase for "cheers," and they swallowed the formaldehyde-laced brew with gusto.

"Why did you say that, Eli?"

"What, *gan bei*?"

"No - that both our goals should be fulfilled. We have the same goal don't we - to get the statue?"

"Well, let's just say that I have had this feeling all along that there's more to what's been happening than you're telling me." Eli poured two more glasses and waved at the waitress to bring another bottle.

"Now really Eli, I............."

"I know, I know. You've been perfectly honest and told me everything you know. You don't have to repeat it for my benefit. I know the tune by heart. I'm just telling you that I *feel* something else is going on. I've been wrong about things like this before, Lord knows. What can I say? It's the way I feel."

His beautiful employer stared into her glass for a split second and said, "Drink up. It's time for our walk."

Eli's head was spinning from the toxic yellow liquid and he and Mai Lee stumbled unevenly out onto the beach. They doffed their shoes by the path and weaved their way out onto the sand and to a nearby palm grove. The moon was full and glistened on the water like a silver sheet, making the bay look like an impressionist's painting. The surf pounded on the shore, spraying the warm breeze and shrouding the light in a misty haze. The crashing waves slammed Eli's brain relentlessly until he was numb. As drunk as he knew he was, Eli also knew he hadn't felt this relaxed since his early days in Costa Rica. But it was dangerous to do this on a job. Eli knew that, but hadn't yet managed to kick the bad habits he'd picked up in his five sodden years at the beach. Being at the shore so soon after he'd left Costa Rica brought those feelings and insecurities back, and now he was paying the price.

Mai Lee leaned back against one of the trees, her back curving smoothly to fit the curve of the palm. The other guests were in the restaurant or occupied elsewhere, so they had the beach to themselves. The breeze had kicked up and now blew through her hair like the fronds of the trees that surrounded them. She was strikingly beautiful that way, and Eli was overwhelmed by the aroma of her perfume in his nostrils. "So tell me," he mumbled. "How do we get out of this picnic if things suddenly go to hell?"

Mai Lee smiled drunkenly and shook her head. "You have such a way with words. You are so impertinent for an employee, you know." She laughed and swung her hand, jokingly attempting to slap him.

"Well how would you prefer I address you, "Your Royal Highness?"

"With a touch more respect you swine! I do like "Your Royal Highness." She giggled and stifled a yawn. "I would have fired anyone else instantly for half the things you've said to me in the last 24 hours."

Eli leaned against the tree and brought her hand to his forehead. "Oh "Highness," please forgive my transgressions. Now what can you tell me about how we get out of this place in case the world caves in around us?"

The girl turned to face him and whispered, "No, no. No business right now, servant. You must do what your queen wishes."

"And what would that be?" Eli sighed, hoping to humor her.

"You have to kiss me."

"What? I have to kiss you?"

"You heard what I said. Do it."

"Look," Eli stammered, smiling weakly, " I don't mean to be a drag on your party but I need to get a few things straight in my own mind first. Then we can talk about your wishes."

Mai Lee gazed up at Eli coyly and put her finger up to her lips. She was slightly off balance and nearly slid off the tree. "I'll tell you everything you want to know if you just come a bit closer." She reached out to him but with great effort he managed to maintain his distance.

"You don't know what we're supposed to do, do you?" Eli stammered. "You don't have any idea how we're supposed to get out of this place if all hell breaks loose." He fought to hold onto rational thought even though the formaldehyde-alcohol combination was rapidly gaining ground.

"If you come here just a little closer, I'll tell you everything," she sighed warmly. "Wait - I know! I know how to prove myself to you." She dropped her arms and began to undo her blouse. "I guess there's only one way to show you how much you can trust me." Mai Lee unbuttoned the billowy cotton garment and let it flutter in the ocean breeze. Her bra fell to the sand and she pressed herself against Eli's chest, hugging him tightly. The sensation of her warm, firm breasts almost made him lose his mind. He tried to shake his head to signify his disapproval but only succeeded in throwing himself off balance and into her with his full weight. She reached out and pulled him to her hips, pressing into him. Mai Lee breathed loudly and quickly, moaning in almost inaudible tones as she embraced her protector.

"Eli please, I *need* you." She kissed him hard on the mouth and gasped with pleasure.

The pounding waves reverberated in Eli's head like a thousand bass drums making logical thought impossible. He slipped his hand under her skirt. She thrust herself at his hand and moaned.

"So how do we finish this thing?" Eli insisted with his last ounce of willpower.

Mai Lee breathed in rapid gasps, straining at his touch.

"Finish it? You mean me, darling?"

"How do we get out of China?" Eli sighed, slipping his hand onto her again. "Is there a boat, a plane, a car, or what?"

"It's a boat," she moaned hoarsely. "A boat will take us to the Philippines. That's all I know, I swear. Please, don't stop now." At least his curiosity had been satisfied. Mai Lee pushed her hips against Eli's leg repeatedly, moaning and gasping his name, then slid back against the tree and gazed sleepily at him as her pleasure subsided. She grabbed Eli's hand tightly, staring intently into his eyes. Eli bent down as if to kiss her again but instead picked her bra up off the sand and dangled it in front of her. "What are you doing?" she protested drunkenly, swatting at the thing crazily.

"I'm doing us both a small favor and putting you to bed - alone. You'll be happy I did in the morning."

"No I won't!" she shouted. "I order you to take me right now! As your employer, I order you. Get down there on the sand, now!"

"Sorry boss," said Eli unconvincingly. She began to slump against the tree, so Eli shoved her arms through the bra straps and fastened two of the buttons on her shirt. "Time to go." he draped her over his back and half dragged, half carried the girl back to their room. Eli managed to remember their shoes before he got to the lobby, though securing them with the girl on his back took the last bit of focus he had.

"Oh Eli, I don't feel so good." Mai Lee's face suddenly turned ashen white and her closed eyes opened wide. "I think I will be sick now," she whispered formally, and slumped to her knees by the path. She knelt there in the sand, heaving and coughing while Eli wiped her face with the few tissues he had in his pocket. After she'd regained control of her stomach Eli picked her up and staggered back to the room. "I've made a mess," she mumbled, sobbing faintly as she faded into sleep. "I'm so sorry."

"Relax boss lady, you're just fine."

"But you're counting on me to hold up my end and now look. I'm terrible," she added between the tears.

"Quiet now," said Eli in hushed tones. "We'll start

fresh all over again tomorrow. Now it's time for sleep."
He stumbled into the room and his momentum carried
them over to the bed. Eli dropped the limp girl onto the
sagging mattress as gently as he could and stripped her
clothes off, tossing them in the sink.

"I'm sorry," she mumbled again, and then fell silent.
Eli allowed himself to admire her body for a moment.
Even in his drunken state, the image of her lying naked
on the bed was something he'd carry with him for years
to come. He then covered her as best he could and
shuffled off to the bathroom to wash his face and her
clothes.

Eli was proud he was able to resist her. That gave
him a feeling of confidence that he hadn't had for a
while, since resisting women had always been nearly
impossible for him. He sorely needed a dose of
confidence, more than he needed Mai Lee. Eli rinsed
her shirt and hung it over the shower rod to dry then
took a handful of aspirins and stumbled back to the bed.
His mind drifted off while he tried one last time to
digest what she'd told him. A boat to the Philippines!
Eli needed an alternate plan, one that didn't depend on
her contacts to get them all the way across the South
China Sea. At least he had a few more hours to come up
with something and considering what he'd just had to
endure, he figured that additional task would be no
problem at all.

§

"Wake up sleepy head," said Eli, shaking her naked shoulder briskly. "Time to get going. We haven't got a lot of time left before the rendezvous."

"Oh my God," groaned Mai Lee ominously. "My head is bursting. Please, let me die quietly." The girl pulled the covers over her and jerked her body in surprise, suddenly noticing her nudity.

"Come on, get up," Eli said, slapping the edge of the bed. "You might want to ask me why you're naked but I wouldn't advise it," he said, stifling a grin. "We've got a job to do and that's the only thing we should be thinking about now."

Mai Lee pulled the covers up to her neck and sat up against the headrest while he jammed some aspirins and a glass of water into her hands. "Thanks," she whispered, gulping the little white tablets feebly. "Did I do something frightfully stupid last night?"

"Not that I recall. What do you think you did?" "I can't say exactly," she sighed, "but I remember being sick on the beach. I think it was the beer. I guess I must have made a mess of myself, considering this," she said, looking at herself under the covers. "Did you get a good view?"

"Breathtaking," Eli smiled.

"Right then, please turn round so I can go to the shower. One free peak doesn't mean you're entitled to a free show." Mai Lee smiled feebly and gathered the sheet around herself in a half-hearted manner, so Eli turned around to face the wall. "Now I don't want any cheating," she added, walking to the bathroom. After she had dressed, they grazed on a light *dim sum* breakfast and then hired a taxi for the short ride to Sanya. As they passed the palm shaded fishing settlements that lined the road, Eli was reminded of a saying Mai Lee had told him the natives of Hainan have about Sanya: it may not be the end of the world but you can certainly see it from there.

Their first view of *real* Chinese living, exemplified by the vast differences between westernized towns like Guangzhou and Shanghai and rural areas like Sanya, came into view as the taxi crossed the bridge into the center of town. Every street, every building was in a state of advanced decay or dismemberment. Ongoing sewer and drainage projects had given the city center the appearance of little more than a large pile of rocks surrounded by various crumbling buildings. The taxi driver conveyed the popular government message that they were seeing the new renovation Beijing had promised, designed to significantly enhance the local population's quality of life and boost foreign tourism.

The taxi crawled slowly through the hoards of suicidally-driven pedicabs that clogged the obstructed roads, searching for a clear path to the main outdoor market. The young girls that operated the vile machines had difficulty seeing above the brims of their large flat hats, and they often ran afoul of the slower "iron buffaloes" that crept along like huge snails. The machines were a cross between a tractor and a motorcycle, with long handle bars that resembled the horns of a water buffalo.

The taxi driver let them out in front of the outdoor market, frustrated at his inability to shuttle his passengers to the intersection they wanted. Eli and Mai Lee stood still for a few minutes trying to orient themselves with the poorly copied map they'd secured from Qing Ping Market. "I think it's over there," said Mai Lee pointing down the block. Eli nodded and they walked through the trash briskly, easily outpacing the "iron buffaloes" with their huge loads of wood, bricks, and chickens.

"There - near the bus station." Mai Lee pointed to a corner that resembled the one on the map. "You know, a Tang Dynasty minister named Lee Deyu once said that Hainan Island was "The Gate of Hell." Maybe he understated the situation a bit."

Eli laughed loudly, glad to know his unfavorable impression was not due to his *gwailo* status. "Ok, so what do we do now?"

"We wait," she said impatiently, trying to rub the hangover from her temples. "I think we'll be pretty obvious to anyone that might want to find us."

"I should think so," said Eli, surveying the sad state of the local dress.

They stood on the corner for nearly 40 minutes and saw nothing. "Look, it's almost 11:30. Something has obviously gone wrong and I don't think it's a good idea to stay here any longer. We're too exposed and whoever this local guy is may have run into the same sort of problem as our man in Guangzhou. Let's blow this place while we still have our luck."

"Wait a minute," she blurted out, grabbing his arm. "This looks promising." A large, black Soviet-made ZIL-41047 limousine rolled slowly towards them through the rubble in a way Eli would never have called "promising."

"I don't like this," Eli murmured, fighting the urge to grab the girl and run. The limo slowed beside them and a rear window opened.

"Jones?" called a voice in crisp English.

Mai Lee nodded, and the car door opened to admit them. "Get in quickly," came the order, and Eli followed her into the back of the big car. They sat across from a very well dressed Han Chinese. He smiled thinly, artificially, and eyed the couple for a few seconds before he spoke.

"Miss Jones, Mister........"

"Rose," Eli said flatly. "Eli Rose. And you are.........?"

"My name is Hwang. I will be your eyes and ears for the rest of your quest."

He smiled again and extended his hand, which was clammy and limp to the touch. "Don't you think this is a bit conspicuous for an operative, Mr. Hwang?" Eli said sarcastically.

"Oh, you mean the car? Yes, of course. Well actually, you see it goes with the job. I am the chief of the Communist Party here in Sanya District. The car and driver have been put at my disposal so I see no reason why I should not use them."

"Mr. Hwang, you obviously know quite a bit about us so forgive me for being blunt. Uncle said you would be able to arrange for us to secure the statue from here. When can we conclude our business?"

"My dear girl, spending so much time in the West must have affected your manners." Hwang poured three small cups of Mao Tai from his amply stocked bar and handed them over carefully. "First we must toast this successful meeting and our future profitable negotiations." He raised his cup and tossed the clear liquid down in one swallow.

"*Gan bei*," said Eli, following his lead. Mai Lee winced at the smell of the alcohol but drank it anyway. "What do you mean negotiations?" Eli added.

"Perhaps I should not consider you uncultured," he answered, evading Eli's question. Hwang stroked his thin hair effeminately, smiling like a department store mannequin.

"Perhaps it is unwise to underestimate one's friends," replied Eli, putting the cup on the bar.

"Quite right," he laughed. "Our arrangement calls for me to escort you personally to where we will regain possession of your merchandise. However, my expenses have been somewhat greater than I anticipated when I agreed to this venture and those "fees" will need to be recovered."

Mai Lee frowned but remained calm. "Mr. Hwang, we have a deal. However, we are not unreasonable and if you truly have had expenses beyond your original estimate, I'm certain we can work something out."

The skinny guy smiled and nodded. "Precisely why I said we must still negotiate the final price for my work."

"Ok. Let's talk about what comes next," Eli interjected.

"Well, my dear Mr. Rose, we are presently driving to Xincun to meet some special friends of mine. They are one of the reasons my expenses have increased but as you will soon see, the additional funds were well worth it." Hwang straightened the cuffs of his shirt sleeves so that they extended exactly the same distance beyond his coat on each arm. "From Xincun we will go to Haikou and then travel by ferry to the Mainland. We will then drive to Nanning to recover your artifact."

"We need to stop by the hotel and........," said Mai Lee.

"Your things are already in the trunk, packed and cleaned for the trip, my dear," hissed Hwang. "That is what delayed us a bit this morning." The ZIL bounced out of town along the dusty coast road and turned north, heading inland. Hwang offered a second drink which his guests politely declined. He smiled and closed the bar. "Now then, I believe Mr. Rose would like to ask me some questions. Am I correct, Mr. Rose?"

"Yes," Eli said coldly. "Let's start with you. You seem to have everything you could want here - why risk it all for a few *Yuan*?"

"Very simple, Mr. Rose - we are not talking about just a few *Yuan*. Mr. Cheung has agreed, with some recent modifications, to pay me $50,000 U.S. This money will provide me with something that is in short supply in China, even for officials of my stature."

"And what would that be?"

"Freedom, Mr. Rose. The freedom to leave this

place and begin again in a new country with enough money to invest in the right business opportunity. It is true that I live much better than the average person in this country but I do not have much to look forward to. The best I could expect would be a small government pension and a small apartment in Guangzhou, full of small things of little value. I want *more* from life, *much more*."

"Go on," said Eli, "I'm not stopping you."

"Mr. Cheung has generously suggested that I might be employed with his firm in Canada. The offer is too good to refuse."

"Mr. Hwang, I do believe you're a capitalist," Eli said pointedly.

"Let us just say that I believe in seizing opportunities when they arise." The car continued on for a few silent minutes before Eli asked the $50,000 question.

"Just one more thing. How do we get our hands on the item in question?"

Hwang grimaced, contorting his face plastically at an odd angle. "Really, Mr. Rose. If I told you that what would you need me for? All in good time. Our first order of business is to travel to Bei Hai as quickly as possible so that our local guides do not get nervous and ruin all our grand plans."

"Fair enough," Eli replied. "Mr. Cheung also said I would be able to acquire a weapon nearby. I would like to do that as soon as possible."

"Certainly, Mr. Rose. I will alert you when we are close to the supplies Mr. Cheung has graciously made available to you."

The plan was once again too vague for Eli's tastes. Relying extensively on Hwang's slippery word that everything had been smoothly planned out was too much of a risk. Eli was determined to make the little clown jump at some point, since it was critical to find out just how much his well-oiled machine could handle when something happened that wasn't part of the plan.

Chapter 10

The arrival of a ZIL limousine in Xincun was an uncommon sight to say the least. It made the presence of one high official of the Communist Party and two obviously wealthy foreigners in the sleepy fishing village less than subtle. A gawking crowd of curious townspeople boiled out of every shop and open window to see the important official, the rich girl and the *gwailo* in the big, black limo. The locals stared at them as if they were from Mars; as far as the islanders were concerned it was more a more likely circumstance than if their new guests were from the west. The crowd followed them down to the docks like a flock of sheep.

Hwang cursed in Cantonese as he cleared the sand from his Gucci loafers and pushed his way through the locals. "It will be only a few more minutes before the boat arrives," he snarled, cursing at the people to leave and waving his arms. The crowd continued to press onto the rotten wooden structure, seriously threatening to collapse it and soak the lot of them. Hwang continued to curse at them until they shouted back and began to disperse. "These people are swine," he sniffed, pouring another pile of sand from his shoe. Eli surveyed the town carefully but came away with a different impression.

Though the buildings were in a similar state as those in Sanya he was impressed by the relative cleanliness of the beach and the people. The local people were boat builders as well as fishermen and their brightly painted sampans appeared to be well constructed and ready for action. Life in Xincun seemed simple, much the same as in Playa Coco. Things probably hadn't changed much in a thousand years and Eli doubted whether Mao and his *Cultural Revolution* were anything more than dim memories here. The air was warm and salty and the sun baked the trio mercilessly while they waited for their transportation.

Hwang paced and fidgeted nervously with his hands, making it look like he was giving himself a manicure. Eli allowed his attention to wander off to Monkey Island with its dwindling primate population. He wondered how many of the local population still ate the little beasts. Mai Lee had pulled Hwang aside during Eli's momentary lapse and was in the process of berating him in Cantonese when the roar of a distant engine broke in to interrupt them. The three stared back towards the far side of the island and soon the large rooster tail of prop wash common in offshore racers came into view.

"There we are, there we are," stuttered Hwang with relief. "I told you they would be here," he said sarcastically to Mai Lee. She turned her back on him and walked back to Eli.

"Mr. Hwang this is not exactly what I expected," Eli exclaimed as the jet black bullet zoomed closer.

"Yes, I am certain you didn't," he replied with a smile. "This beauty was custom built. It has two large American engines, the very best. I believe we can reach a speed of 120 kilometers per hour on a calm sea." He folded his arms, satisfied with his demonstration of technical knowledge. "Oh yes, "he added quickly. "We seized it from drug smugglers that were operating between the Philippines and our southern ports. Quite a nice prize, don't you think?"

"It's a real gem. How long to Haikou from here?"

"If all goes well perhaps three and a half hours." The boat slowed as it approached the dock and settled in next to them. The two-man crew motioned them aboard after stowing their things in the small cargo area, and the group settled into the comfortable seats for the rest of the day. The speed boat roared through the warm coastal waters as Hwang insisted upon explaining in great detail, why the overland route was too time consuming and too dangerous. "The traffic accidents are too much of a risk," he shouted. "Many people are killed each year on the Wenchang to Haikou road because they cannot obey the rules."

"How tragic," Eli said bluntly.

"Quite," was the unemotional reply. The sea was unusually calm and their approach into the port of Haikou was uneventful and smooth. They motored slowly up the harbor channel and moored at the military dock, just behind a rusted coastal gunboat. "Please follow me," said the skinny guy, ushering Eli and Mai Lee into another ZIL limo. "We will drive to the ferry and take my car to Bei Hai."

The drive was brief but frenetic due to the multitudes of bicyclists that clogged the road to the ferry landing. The vibration of the boat's powerful engines still echoed through Eli's legs when they arrived and he was relieved to be able to get out and survey the old boat, if only for the opportunity to stretch. They had managed to arrive just in time to catch the last boat to the Mainland and were under way in a matter of minutes. The timing was perfect; almost too perfect. Eli was concerned that he might be looking for a plot where there wasn't one. He ignored the feeling and relaxed as Haikou slipped from view.

Mai Lee walked over to the rear deck to watch the sampans sail past them, rocking in the ferry's boiling wake. Eli decided to join her and just listen to what she had to say. The girl was much less guarded around him now and the chance to learn more of the truth was too good to pass up. "I have to say that I won't miss this place at all," he said.

"I agree," she answered quietly.

Eli looked at the beautiful girl standing beside him,

her hair blowing gracefully in the breeze and pulled her close, kissing the top of her head. "Come on now. It sounds like you're sad to leave. After all, what could be the problem? We're finally on our way. This whole thing will be over in one or two more days, tops."

"I know," she sighed. After a short pause she pulled away and stared up at Eli with a steely serious look in her big eyes. "Eli, I have to tell you something very important. You've been right to doubt me all this time. There really is something I haven't told you. I............"

"Yes," Eli said expectantly. "Go on."

"Yes, do continue Miss Jones," added Hwang sarcastically from over Eli's shoulder. "Please don't let me interrupt you."

Mai Lee cursed him tersely in Mandarin and stalked off towards the bow in a whirlwind of flowing black hair. "She is a bit high strung, don't you think?" said Hwang.

"I wouldn't know," Eli replied coldly. "She's never done that before." Hwang smiled dryly and retreated to the passenger area while Eli wandered the deck.

Lunch was being prepared and served, and on the ferry it was a highly informal affair and best observed rather than consumed. The crew was cooking at various locations aboard the big ship and the group near the wheelhouse had a large stew pot boiling for all who wished to partake. Eli politely declined so they voraciously snapped up the brown and gray chunks of meat with their clicking chop sticks, barely stopping for a breath. Eli thought that they might even eat Hwang if he'd been cut up and stewed long enough. The skinny guy exited as unceremoniously as he'd entered, and the void created by Mai Lee's absence left Eli with a bitter aftertaste, like the skin of a raw plum. He looked out at the horizon and watched the sun grow fat and orange as it slipped through the low-hanging clouds.

The unpleasant possibility that he could be falling in love with the girl was a prospect Eli dreaded like poison. The inconvenience of such strong feelings would constantly work against his better judgment and he thought seriously about shutting her down at the very next opportunity. Unfortunately for him that tactic hadn't worked before, so he was at a loss for new ideas.

Eli continued to gaze out at the darkening sky until the bedraggled port of Xuwen materialized in the purple twilight. A stiff breeze swept in off the ocean and chilled him suddenly, making the hair on the back of his neck bristle. Eli sensed, even smelled trouble on the coming moonrise and it seemed time to force the action before something worse occurred. He hoped that Mai Lee would pick up his lead quickly.

He was definitely infatuated with the girl, and even though he wasn't sure how deep his feelings went, he hoped he wouldn't have to choose between leaving her behind and losing his advantage, if he was able to secure one. Eli decided that he'd wait until the last possible moment to make that choice. The ferry pulled up to the dock with a jolt and the trio went back down to the car to start the long drive to Bei Hai. He crossed his fingers and prayed that his luck and judgment would hold up even though his heart had betrayed him.

§

The big ZIL rolled out of the ferry with a silent, tired set of occupants. Mai Lee stared out the window at the small hovels that flew past in the dim headlights and said nothing. Hwang sat in the front next to the driver and chatted quietly with him in Mandarin, something Eli thought strange but not too unusual. They seemed to debate the route from time to time as they passed various road signs but always sounded amicable, almost friendly.

"Mr. Rose, we are going to sleep in Bei Hai tonight but it will be very late before we arrive."

"That's fine with me Mr. Hwang," Eli lied. "Let's just do whatever it takes to finish the job and get on with it."

"Quite right, quite right."

The old car bumped along for two more hours through the desolate, dark countryside. Eli was somewhat surprised that the area was so sparsely populated, a real oddity for China considering the massive number of inhabitants, and the emptiness added to his growing feeling of discomfort. A strange sense of being watched began to hit Eli and he looked over his shoulder, half expecting to see someone standing on the bumper. Instead he managed a fleeting glimpse of two sets of headlights far to the rear. "We will need to pull off the main road for a few miles," announced Hwang abruptly. "The driver has told me that recent storms have washed away the road just ahead and we must divert until we can rejoin the good part."

Eli was alarmed and certain that something bad was about to happen. "Listen Mr. Hwang, do you think you could pull over at that small store for a minute before we leave this road? I need to relieve myself."

"Certainly," he said in a measured tone. Mai Lee looked squarely into his bloodshot eyes for a second and then looked away. She still refused to look at Eli, who couldn't tell whether she'd remembered their little tango at the beach and was angry or if she just couldn't stand to be around their uncouth little guide.

Civilization in that part of China was defined by a small collection of naked light bulbs in the darkness, and a tiny roadside store that catered to truck drivers and the thin local population. The limo pulled in and Eli jumped out quickly, trying to draw as much attention to their arrival as possible. Hwang glared at him but said nothing and stood next to the car while Eli searched the tiny shop for a bathroom.

The decaying place was lit by three firefly-sized bulbs suspended by wires in the center of the open room. A small crowd of about 20 people huddled around an old Russian-made black and white television, gawking with open mouths at the blurred images on the tiny screen. "Hello," Eli announced, intending to appear stupid. "Does anyone here speak any English?"

Nineteen dumbfounded stares greeted this question but one voice from the back replied, "Yes. I have some English, yes."

"Can I please speak with you for a minute?"

The bespectacled little man shuffled out to meet Eli and smiled broadly, looking back at his stunned friends with a self important grin. He shook Eli's hand limply and motioned for them to go to another room. The old guy slipped along in his worn sandals, barely lifting his feet as he walked. His twisted features bespoke a life of hard labor but his deep wrinkles and crinkled smile put Eli immediately at ease. He wiped his glasses on his holey white undershirt and smiled at his visitor. "Yes Mister? I can help you?"

"Yes you can. Do you have a map of this area?"

"Map?" he repeated with a puzzled look. Then his expression cleared. "Map - ah yes, map. Yes."

"You have a map? Can I see the map?"

"No map. Sorry, no have," he said shaking his head. Noticing Eli's disappointment he quickly added, "I know area. Live here many year."

"Ok that's great. I need to know if this road is Ok and if there is another road to Bei Hai."

The little man thought for a second and said, "Yes, this road good. Is Ok to Bei Hai. I think we have no other road." That confirmed Eli's growing suspicion of Hwang's transparent deception but he had no idea why the guy cared to lie to him. Maybe there was something on that road he didn't want Eli to see? As a good party official it would stand to reason that he'd want to keep certain things from Eli's view, but he was still uncomfortable with that explanation.

"What is on this road, away from this place near Bei Hai?" Eli asked. "Do you have police or army camp? Do you know?"

"Yes, yes. Police, many police." He pointed down the road for emphasis. "They ask for papers. They stop everyone. You have travel pass?"

"Yes," Eli nodded. That had to be it. Hwang was off his turf without a travel permit, something that would land him in hot water with Beijing if he was caught. No wonder he wanted to detour around to another road.

The little man stole a look around Eli's arm at Hwang and asked, "Who that man?"

"He says his name is Hwang," Eli said. "He is the Party Chief for Hainan."

The little old guy became unusually agitated and quietly said, "No. Not him. Party Chairman for Hainan is..... cousin of my wife brother. Name Chiao, not Hwang."

"Damn!" Eli exclaimed aloud. *How could I have been so damn stupid*, he thought? *He's a bad guy! No wonder he can't get stopped by the cops - they'd fry him quick and send him straight to Mongolia. Hell, they might just shoot him right there for impersonating a party official.*

Eli's new friend nodded, noting his concern. "*Xie, xie*," Eli sighed, shaking the old guy's hand. "You have been a very great help to me." Eli fished around in his pocket for a gift, but all he could find was a set of nail clippers he'd never used. "Please, take this as appreciation for your help."

"Ah, very nice. You very welcome." The old guy smiled and accepted the instrument with pride, then turned and said, "You be careful. He bad man." Eli glanced back at him as he left and waved as his curious friends admired his gift. Hwang or whatever his name really was had pulled the car down the road away from the lights of the store. The whole thing suddenly made so much sense.

"I was beginning to worry about you Mr. Rose," he said with interest.

"Yes, I'm sure you were very concerned with my welfare Mr. Hwang. I just had a few translation problems."

"Quite. We can leave now?"

Eli nodded and reached into his pocket for a ball-point pen. He'd lost hope of getting hold of a real weapon, so this would have to do. As the driver pulled out onto the road, Eli remembered his training during his stay with *El Grupo* in Miami, how they'd taught him to kill with the simple thing he held tightly in his right hand. Mai Lee glared nervously at Hwang and shot a look back to Eli that was too obvious to ignore. "Mr. Hwang," Eli said calmly, pulling the pen out to show the girl "is there anything you wish to tell me before we go any further?"

"No," he said flatly. "Why do you ask?"

"Oh, you know how curious I am." Eli moved the pen point to the back of his neck as Mai Lee's eyes popped with fear. "Besides, I believe that friends should be honest with one another at all times, don't you? Lately I've been feeling a bit unloved and out in the cold."

Hwang swiveled to look at Eli, exasperation in his eyes. "I do not understand. What is......," and Eli grabbed him around the neck with his left arm, compressing his windpipe and exposing his jugular vein. At the same moment Eli brought the point of the pen to his throat, actually puncturing the skin enough to draw a trickle of blood. The suddenness of his attack caused the greasy little rodent to lurch backwards and shriek, which made the driver swerve wildly across the road. Mai Lee jumped but stayed calm and quiet.

"What..........What are you doing?" gasped Hwang.

"Shut up! Tell the driver to pull over NOW or I'll kill you." Eli applied more pressure on the end of the pen to get the point across, so to speak. Hwang spat the order to the driver and the limo skidded to a stop on the dusty shoulder. "Out!" Eli shouted and they slid as one through the open door. Mai Lee and the driver followed, watching intently.

"Eli, what's wrong?" cried Mai Lee.

"This friend of yours, your uncle's contact man is a fake." Eli twisted him violently around to face her and he gasped in fear. "He's one of *them*, one of Old Tiger's men playing some kind of game. Maybe he's trying to catch something from both sides." Eli twisted the little guy down towards the ground to gain better control of him. "What do you have to say about it *friend*?" He jabbed the pen backward slightly for emphasis and Hwang gulped hard, breathing in rapid staccato bursts.

"Eli, no!" yelled Mai Lee. The driver started toward Eli but he squeezed again and Hwang shouted for him to stop.

"Mai Lee, we've got no choice. You have to listen to me - this whole thing has smelled from the very start. We've been set up for some reason but I can't tell you what's happening just yet. For now we have no choice............Search this bastard and see if he has a gun."

The girl sifted through Hwang's pockets gingerly and quickly produced a .25 caliber pistol and held it up to show Eli. He grabbed the little guy and twisted him down hard to his left this time. "Ok, now let's you and I move real slowly back to the car and we'll dump your friend here." Eli started back up towards the car with the pen at Hwang's windpipe and his body between his own and the driver's. "Mai Lee, get in and start the car." Eli couldn't see her from his position but there was no answer. He turned just a bit to look for her and felt the shockingly cold barrel of the .25 against his left ear.

"I'm so sorry Eli," she sobbed. The girl held the pistol with both hands, tears streaming down her beautiful face, gleaming in the moonlight. "I'm sorry...........I have no choice." Hwang began to relax and move but Eli forced him back one last time before releasing him. The snake twisted himself free and immediately straightened his clothes. He calmly took the gun from Mai Lee who began to cry and shake openly and pointed the business end at Eli while the driver held him from behind.

"So Mr. Rose," coughed Hwang, "you think you are so smart but you see now that you know nothing." He leaned over and kissed Mai Lee on top of the head and then swung the gun across Eli's right temple. His head snapped back like a sling shot and he collapsed to his knees, woozy and dazed from the blow. Eli could still think but his head throbbed like he'd been kicked by a horse. "Yes, you must have guessed I am not an official of "The Party." The little weasel laughed loudly. "So yes, I do work for the Old Tiger but also for Mr. Cheung."

Eli's head began to clear and he managed to ask,

"Right, but how is that possible? Why would you take that kind of a risk?"

Hwang laughed again and shook his head, "Oh Mr. Rose, perhaps I gave you too much credit. You really do not understand, do you?" Eli was silent, trying to regain his equilibrium and didn't care to exert the effort to answer him. "Well there is a commodity for exchange here Mr. Rose...and you have now become the prize." Eli looked up at him, bleary-eyed and aching, unable to understand what he meant. "You see, there is a new deal. Instead of buying back the statue for cash, Mr. Cheung has agreed to "sell" you to Old Tiger for the statue. Miss Jones was sent along to ensure your cooperation with the transaction. Unfortunately you discovered too much of our business before the deal was consummated. Such a pity."

"Why does he want *me*?"

Hwang chuckled and shook his head. "I understand it has something to do with your previous line of work, as well as an old score he wishes to settle with you. It is not my business to ask too many questions; it's not a healthy practice. But now you have made my job more difficult." He walked over to the driver and mumbled something to him while Eli managed to wobble to his feet. The cars that had been following them finally pulled up along the highway and disgorged a small army of poorly dressed thugs. They stood around Eli in a semi-circle, staring silently. Eli looked unsteadily at Mai Lee who sobbed quietly when she caught his gaze.

"Why all this?" Eli croaked. "Why the big game, the big tour? All the phony hits, all those lives.........Why do all that?"

"Because of your reputation Mr. Rose," spat Hwang. "You are a very dangerous man." His high-pitched laugh made him sound like a rooster. "We were given to understand that you would never have cooperated even this much had you smelled something rotten, shall we say. We were specifically instructed to deliver you as undamaged as possible and this was the best way to make certain that was possible. Otherwise," he smiled, "I'm afraid we would have had to "damage" you."

"I knew it was too good to be true," Eli stammered. He glared at Mai Lee who turned her face away with a sharp jerk to avoid him. "It was all a lie, wasn't it? Damn, I was such a fool to think..........."

"No, no!" she shouted through her tears.

"How touching," mused Hwang. "Enough of this. Let's get going." Eli reached out feebly for Mai Lee but felt a sharp thud on the back of his head. As he fell forward into the darkness, Eli could clearly recall reaching out to her as the tears ran down her sweet face.

Chapter 11

A day and half passed in a haze of confused and blurred images. Abstract views of faces and voices filled his head with odd combinations of Mandarin and English. Eli's mind repeatedly drifted from sleep to dim consciousness. When he was lucid he cursed himself for not realizing the trap sooner. When he was groggy there was only a strong sense of motion, of having been carried around from one place to the next and of the familiar, ugly face of Hwang.

He had no memory of having seen Mai Lee during that time. One day, Eli wasn't sure exactly when, his vision began to clear and he finally awoke to the image of a blank gray wall. The paint had peeled away in large sheets and the surface heaved with ugly boils and cracks.

"So Mr. Rose, you are rejoining us. That is good." Hwang leaned in close and grinned and Eli grabbed weakly for his throat before he realized that his hands and feet had been bound to the bed posts. "Oh what a shame," he said sarcastically. "It seems that someone has restrained you. But of course it was done for your protection. You will have to learn some self control for the near future my friend."

"I was drugged?" Eli asked, slurring the words.

"Quite. It made things much easier on us."

"How long?

"Two days," said Hwang as he paced in front of the bed.

Eli twisted and pulled at the leather straps to secure some relief from the restriction of his circulation. "Listen, I've got to go to the toilet."

"Really? And you will actually use it this time?" *This time*? Eli had no idea what he meant. Hwang motioned for the straps to be untied and Eli sat up unsteadily and swung his numb legs off the bed while one of the guards untied his arms. "We will have someone to escort you this time. The last time we allowed you to relieve yourself you gave one of our fellows a nasty crack on the head. Now behave yourself or we will have to put you under again."

"Where is Mai Lee?" Eli shouted, weaving drunkenly down the hall.

"We can discuss the girl later," he called after his groggy prisoner.

Eli stretched and rubbed his wrists and ankles briskly, trying to force some feeling back into them before he had to be strapped down again. The small fragment of glass that served as a bathroom mirror revealed his dirty, unshaven face and the blood stains in his hair. Eli rinsed his pounding head in the slimy sink and returned to his escort, who walked him back to the bedroom. Hwang was not there and the guard left Eli alone to go find him. The door was unlocked and unguarded, a trick Eli had seen before. It was often used as a means to frustrate escape attempts and break a prisoner's will by easy and frequent recapture. But his life depended on any opportunity so knowing it was a trap didn't seem to make a difference. Soon, Eli was bobbling and stumbling his way down the hall. The front door of the house was open and he could smell the tepid outside air, luring him to continue on. He fell through the door and onto a lawn of newly mown grass, and was quickly surrounded by a dozen heavily armed men. "So glad you could join us for tea," called Hwang from across the lawn. Eli could barely make out the fuzzy forms of three people sitting under an open air gazebo, and one of them waved as he strained to focus. "Come on, come on. It's alright; we're waiting."

Eli dragged himself up and made a bold attempt to walk normally over to the small group. As he neared the gathering he could finally discern the faces of Hwang and Mai Lee, though the third was unfamiliar to him. "Sit my friend," said Hwang with mock concern. He pulled out a chair for Eli. "Sit and have some tea and biscuits with us."

Eli fell into the chair without acknowledging Mai Lee and gulped the hot liquid. He devoured the biscuits as fast as he could while his three hosts watched. His stomach quickly settled and allowed him to concentrate on the stranger. "Please allow me to introduce your new host, the honorable General Sho of the Independent People's Militia. He will be escorting you to the territory of your new master. Be a good fellow and say hello, won't you?"

Eli was still focused on the tea, but he managed to scald Mai Lee with a blistering stare that nearly brought her to tears. "Now that's no way to behave," said Hwang quietly. He waved at someone behind Eli who then stepped up and hit him sharply in the back with a short bamboo pole. Eli winced and grunted an acknowledgement.

"You see General, he is a bit testy. Don't relax your guard for one moment - he might bite you. I suggest you drug him for the rest of your trip."

"No. We need him to ride so he must be in good condition." The General stared at Eli like he was a barnyard animal ready for the slaughterhouse, "Yes, I think he will be ready to travel soon."

"May I leave now?" whispered the girl.

"Miss Jones, you don't mean to tell me that spending more time with our friend here is upsetting to you? How fickle women are.......You just cannot trust them, can you Mr. Rose?"

"Let's get this over with," Eli said hoarsely. He could finally concentrate on something other than the food and drink but he still had little energy. The drugging had sapped every ounce of strength from him and he badly needed some time to recover.

Mai Lee started to say something to Eli but

suddenly thought better of it and stopped herself abruptly. "I'll get my things," she sighed. Eli watched her walk away and then got up from the table to sit on the grass nearby.

The General shouted several sets of orders to the men who began to assemble their equipment on the lawn in front of them. Their transportation into the jungle was marched out as well - 15 small Khazak horses, with several pack horses as spares. Each of the men carried new versions of the Chinese-made AK-47, the Type 81, with two bandoleers of ammunition strapped across their chests. Eli knew these rifles by reputation as good, reliable weapons. But with their horses, small field packs, and ragged uniforms they looked more like a part of Pancho Villa's army than some modern mechanized infantry. The men themselves were not Chinese but rather mountain tribesmen from Cambodia and Vietnam. They gathered quietly in a business-like and efficient manner and Eli realized that he'd have no choice but to meet the man behind the scenes and find out why he was wanted so badly.

The travelers mounted their horses without ceremony while the bald General shook hands with Hwang, who waved at Eli and smiled. "It has been a pleasure Mr. Rose. Best wishes for a short future." He laughed and disappeared inside the house with his bodyguards. The General shouted at his men and the group trudged off into the jungle.

§

"Hey General, how about untying my hands for awhile?" Eli called out. He rode on without acknowledging Eli's request, riding stiffly in his English saddle like he was made of wood. The ropes cut into Eli's wrists and bent around the saddle horn in a painful loop, twisting his hands at an odd angle. "Come on General. You don't want to deliver damaged goods to your boss, do you?"

The stern figure riding at the head of the column suddenly raised his riding crop and shouted for the group to stop. Sho wheeled his tiny horse around and galloped briskly up to where Eli sat. "Shanyi!" he shouted. "Cut him loose!" He glared at Eli while a disheveled young kid of 18 ran up and cut the ropes. Eli looked at the kid, who seemed genuinely terrified of his commander and realized that money was not the only motivation for people in this army. "You will be quiet now," grunted the General and he galloped back to the head of the column.

Eli rubbed his aching wrists to life as they bumped along the path, one horse following the other as if they were connected on a wire. Eli's head still spun from the drugs and the unbelievable heat and humidity really beat him down. Mai Lee was soaked in sweat and her naked back stuck transparently to her shirt as she rode silently with the bald tyrant. The column continued on for hours through the dense, overhanging bamboo forest, dodging the interwoven razor grass that grew in thickets along the trail. Any encounter with the grass resulted in bloody cuts and shredded clothes. The narrow path meandered through rock-lined streams, up hills and down into stream-filled valleys. Eli remembered seeing pictures and descriptions of this area from his old CIA buddies and he guessed they had passed into the northern part of Vietnam; not his first choice for a vacation destination.

As the group crested the top of a high hill the General shouted for the column to stop and dismount. "We rest here 30 minutes," he shouted back to Eli, who jumped off his sweaty mount. Eli was quickly ushered over to the General and pushed down to a sitting position with the butt of a rifle. Mai Lee and the General sipped mineral water and enjoyed the slight breeze that trickled through the treetops while Eli looked on, dry and exhausted. "Have some water, Mr. Rose," offered the General politely, handing the bottle to Eli. He gulped down a large swallow, unconcerned with the amount or the General's reaction. "No problem," Sho laughed. "We have more. I hope you are feeling better now."

Eli looked at him blankly and said, "We must be getting close to home. Why else would you be so concerned with my well-being?"

"You are quite right sir. But I also admit that I have some admiration for you. Your reputation is well known to me."

"Yeah, it seems my reputation is *too* well known."

"That is the price of success in one's business endeavors, Mr. Rose," laughed the General. Eli stared out across the rolling countryside and tried to get a better sense of exactly where they were.

"Back there in that valley is Ningming?" Eli queried innocently.

Sho pointed to the north and replied, "We are now five kilometers inside Vietnam territory and three kilometers from our destination, there." The crisply appointed man nodded ahead at a tree-covered valley. Mai Lee sat in front of Eli and stared distantly at the horizon, appearing to be lost in thought. The General asked her several times if she wanted more water but she never replied, continuing to concentrate on the horizon. "We go now," announced the old man and the sweat-soaked group slowly mounted their horses for the final few kilometers. Eli realized that escape was virtually impossible in the present situation. In fact, he began to realize that his alternatives were running out and that he might have to consider a desperate rather than a calculated move to get himself some distance from the group.

They rode on into the steaming valley as the local monkey population chattered and shouted at them from the trees. The jungle was strangely quiet otherwise, save for the occasional parrot they surprised in the underbrush. The camp appeared abruptly as the column reached the top of a small, tree-shrouded hill, carved meticulously from the surrounding jungle as if it had been etched in granite. Eli was still a bit dizzy from the lack of sufficient food and water but was able to concentrate better on the details as the group approached. He could see two guard towers at the front of the compound with one man in each. The border fence seemed to be electrified and the mounded area in front of it suggested a small mine field. There were four - no, five buildings and some small storage sheds scattered throughout the camp. Depending upon the number of buildings that served as dormitories, Eli guessed that the compound housed about 100 men. He mumbled to himself that he was in very deep.

"What was that, Mr. Rose?" asked the General.

"Oh, nothing. Just thinking aloud." The column headed for the main gate, a bamboo and concertina wire contraption reminiscent of a World War II jungle prison camp. They crossed through an open assembly area and passed into the center of the compound, a square surrounded by four large tin-roofed barracks. General Sho ordered the column to dismount and Eli was immediately seized by two of the guards and shoved forward. "Let me warn you to show the proper respect or you will be very sorry." The General straightened his uniform as the door immediately ahead of them burst open. Two guards strode out and hustled quickly over to the General, stopping rigidly beside him. The man that emerged from the barracks was not at all what Eli had expected.

Old Tiger bounded out through the doorway and across the square to where the sweat-soaked group waited. His khaki uniform and stern, hammered features reminded Eli of Colonel Saito, the tyrannical Japanese prison camp commander from the movie, "*Bridge Over the River Kwai*", except that this was no movie. Where was Alec Guinness when you needed him?

"Ah Mr. Rose. So very nice of you to join us. And the lovely Miss Jones - always a pleasure. You are as beautiful as the last time we met." He turned coldly to the General and said, "That will be all General Sho. You are dismissed." Old Tiger saluted him and the General bowed low, turned smartly on his heels and ordered his men to disperse. The new guards flanked Eli instantly as the tired column headed off to the cook shack, where a line had formed for the evening meal. "Please my friends, follow me." The smiling old man led Eli and Mai Lee into his quarters and they followed slowly, mindful of the General's warning. "Please, please, come in and relax. Ngyuon, fetch some drinks for our guests." The servant bowed low and ran off to the bar.

"This is very impressive, sir. Air conditioning in the jungle - that's quite a trick." Eli surveyed the well-appointed building carefully and quickly spotted a large green statue mounted on a pedestal in the corner.

Old Tiger smiled and motioned for the couple to sit in some white rattan chairs that faced him. "Yes, but not impossible as you can clearly see. Nothing is impossible here." The servant entered the room with a tray of drinks and offered the first to the old man. "Perrier with a twist of lime. I hope that will be refreshing to you. We can save the wine for dinner." Eli and Mai Lee gulped the drinks rapidly and the old man motioned for Ngyuen to bring another for each. "Yes, the weather here can be quite draining if you're not accustomed to it."

"Look Mister Old Tiger, I don't know what you want with me so why don't we just cut the suspense and get to the point."

The old man glared at Eli coldly with coal-black eyes that projected great malevolence. He forced a smile and sighed. "In time you will come to know why I have spared no expense to bring you here. As for you my dear Mai Lee, your uncle and I have a new understanding. Is that correct?"

"I was told that a deal had been made," she said coldly.

"Ah yes, a deal. Let me show you around my humble facility and then perhaps we'll talk business. You may come too, Mr. Rose." They walked out onto the rear wooden deck that attached directly to the bungalow and Eli realized why Old Tiger was so feared by those that opposed him. Across the small ravine that ran below the bungalow was a small hilltop landing strip, hidden from view by camouflage netting. Five Soviet MI-24A Hind helicopter gunships sat under the cover like large, vicious dragon flies ready for action. A fuel depot sat nearby and the entire area was surrounded by SAM anti-aircraft batteries. Eli was even able to discern what appeared to be an early warning radar installation on a distant hill. "Impressive, don't you think?" he crowed proudly.

"Yes, very," said Eli surveying the scene closely. They walked down the path towards the ravine, the crisply appointed old man showing off his expensive hidden technology and defenses. "This is very impressive sir, but what's the point? Why do you want to defend this miserable piece of ground so badly? No offense intended."

"None taken my boy."

"Why not just move on when the "heat" gets too intense?" Eli stopped to wait for the answer.

"You do not know me, do you Mr. Rose? Miss Jones knows me quite well, don't you my dear?" He smiled smugly at her, but she turned away in disgusted silence. "My dear Mai Lee, you don't wish to tell him about my research?"

She shot back with an angry look as they strolled out across a small foot bridge, and down a path that wound lazily through the thick underbrush. The path followed a small stream around the hill and opened into a tree-lined clearing which revealed a row of modern greenhouses nestled snugly together. "Please, you both must see my current project." Old Tiger opened the door of the first aluminum structure and motioned for them to go inside. "Do you know how much all this cost, Mr. Rose?"

"Let me guess - millions? But I know you're going to tell me anyway, whether I want to know or not."

The old guy laughed and shook his head. "How amusing! Try hundreds of millions. It was very difficult to move all this here, to this remote location. And the research involved in all this is truly cutting edge. But then, my finances were more than adequate when I built all this."

"And your money came from............"

"Opium," he interjected. "Opium has given me a very good lifestyle over the years. In fact you could say that once, I was the king of opium in this part of the world. But nothing lasts forever as they say, and I had to leave the business I worked so hard to develop to others."

"How sad," Eli sneered. "I guess all good things must come to an end sometime."

"You are insolent," Old Tiger replied. "We'll have to deal with that aspect of your character later. As I was saying, I was convinced to liquidate my opium business by the actions of your government. They applied some unusually effective pressure in the right places so I decided it was best to retire for awhile. Fortunately, I've found something with much greater growth potential." Mai Lee looked at Eli with raised eyebrows, indicating her surprise and ignorance of the matter.

"These little beauties," said Old Tiger, caressing a small plant tenderly. "A cross between *Erythroxylum coca* and *Erythroxylum novogranatense* - the common coca plant. But these beauties are anything but common Mr. Rose. These form the basis of my newest enterprise."

Old Tiger smiled and studied his guests to gauge their reactions. "I can see from your expressions that you don't recognize what you're viewing, so allow me to enlighten you." He strode off a few paces and turned toward the couple, grinning broadly. "I call it *supercoca*, Mr. Rose, *supercoca*." The old man noted with amusement the looks of total confusion on the faces of his "guests."

"Ah, so you are confused. Let me explain." Old Tiger stretched out his arms and waved at the vast garden behind him. "What is this thing called *supercoca* you ask? These beauties are the new superstars of the narcotics world my friends. I have managed to breed a plant that will produce a variety of coca not found in South America, one that is ten times more powerful and a plant that can be grown under only special conditions here in the "Golden Triangle."

Eli stared in disbelief, inspecting the plants closely as he tried to comprehend what it all meant. "How is this possible? Coca has never been grown successfully outside the main growing areas of the Andes."

"Quite right, my boy. And it would still be impossible under normal circumstances. But this plant is truly amazing. You see, the trick is to maintain a fairly cool average growing temperature, around 77 degrees Fahrenheit. The real secret here is in the design of the greenhouse. Look at this." The old man punched a large red button on the wall next to him, and the side windows of the greenhouse began to rotate open.

"In this way, I can shade the plants adequately during the day and provide the ventilation they need, while still keeping them warm in the evening." Old Tiger pulled a leaf from one of the nearby stems and held it up in front of the pair. "Our distillation process is also a huge improvement on the crude techniques used in South America, allowing us to better exploit the plant's biochemical characteristics. We can refine a drug that exceeds the power and kick of the typical Andean products. Our product performs somewhat in a time released manner, so to speak. A new drug without many of the side effects of the original, plus much more leaf productivity per acre under cultivation. Truly a breakthrough, don't you think?"

Old Tiger let the leaf fall to the floor and walked slowly back towards the entrance of the greenhouse. Eli and Mai Lee were stupefied and could think of nothing to say.

Ah, so I see you are impressed. Thank you – I'll take your silence as a compliment. I'm very proud of my "children" as you can tell. When I said that this enterprise cost me many hundreds of millions of your dollars I was not exaggerating. I have had the best minds in the new science of genetic engineering working on this project. It has taken me many years and many failures, but now I have this successful cross-breed, and it absolutely thrives here."

Eli sighed and rubbed his chin, depressed at the awful prospect that lay in front of him. He followed Old Tiger out of the greenhouse and onto the path, with Mai Lee close behind.

"Just think of it," the old man said wistfully. "Once I have established full production I will take up the slack from the Colombians when your government finally catches the lot of them. This product will supplant South American cocaine as the choice for discriminating "connoisseurs." Eventually, my cheaper, stronger, higher-quality product will take over the market. Imagine the sales volume...........the possibilities are truly incredible." He closed the greenhouse door behind Mai Lee and started back to the bungalow.

Perfect! That's all he needed. Eli knew he could never let a drug like this reach the West. He would have to find a way to stop Old Tiger from succeeding with his plan, and at the same time find a way to get himself out safely. *No problem*, he mused to himself. *Should be a piece of cake*.

"Old Tiger!" said Eli as the old man walked past him. "What the hell does all this have to do with me? Why am I here?"

The old man sighed and walked back to within inches of Eli's face. "I will decide your fate shortly, Mr. Rose."

That made Eli mad. Oh, sure, he was mad long before the old fart said that, but he'd assumed there was some clear underlying reason for the big charade. Now it just seemed like a random act. Maybe the crazy old guy wanted to make an example of him? Grab a US agent, even an old, used up model just to show his competitors he was back in the game. Eli's blood boiled at the thought. "So what's to stop me from deciding your fate right here, right now?" Eli said quietly, ready to rip the old man's jugular vein from his neck.

"You may try to kill me if you wish," Old Tiger whispered back. "But before you can raise a finger to injure me that man behind you will scatter your brains on the ground." He waved his hand lazily at an unseen figure behind Eli, who heard the unmistakable click of a safety being switched off. "Now then, can we go back for dinner?"

Eli gritted his teeth and forced a smile. "Lead on," he hissed. Mai Lee stayed back to walk beside Eli and shivered suddenly in the cool evening air.

"Eli, you've got to believe me. I didn't know anything about all this." She stared up at him, imploring a response with a sorrowful stare.

"Sure, I believe you. Your credibility is right up there with Gandhi on my all time trustworthy list about now."

"Eli, please listen. You don't understand how it is. I had no choice. They promised me you wouldn't be hurt."

"Well, so far it's a good deal for you, right? You'll get your statue, Old Tiger gets me, I get killed, everything is great. Sounds like a win-win to me"

She grabbed his arm and forced him to look at her. They stopped on the small foot bridge below the bungalow while Old Tiger marched up the steps.

"That's not the way it's supposed to work out. They promised me."

"Ok," Eli shot back. "This is the last time I'm going to ask you. Come clean and tell me just what the hell is going on. I could be hanging by my thumbs in a few minutes, so if you ever intended to be honest with me, you'd better start now!" The girl nodded but looked away, wrestling with the prospect of having to tell the truth. Eli wasn't in the mood to make it easy for her so he grabbed her shoulder and spun her around to face him. "Tell me, damn it! Tell me now, or forget you ever knew me."

She sobbed and shook her head. "I'm sorry. I'm so sorry. It was wrong to do this." The girl stared up at the darkening sky as if looking for divine intervention, then added softly, "You're right about me. You were always right." Eli leaned against the bamboo railing as her story began to unravel.

"Uncle's story was only partly true. There never was another carving, only the one you saw in his room. But this one contains over $50 million in diamonds that were intended for "special uses" by my uncle and his people. Old Tiger doesn't know the diamonds are inside the carving."

"What kind of "special uses" was your uncle planning for them?"

"Uncle has been designated by certain individuals in Hong Kong and the U.S. to purchase weapons for the underground in Old China. The plan was to start a true revolution with that equipment, rather than just protest the government," she said bitterly. "This bastard stole the statue and kept the arms he was supposed to sell to us."

"Until he heard I was working for you, right?"

She dropped her head sadly and nodded. "He said that he would go through with the original deal if Uncle would send you here. All this wasn't supposed to happen. He said he just wanted to talk to you, to work out some old debts. I didn't know why he wanted you here"

"But something else got in the way, didn't it?" Eli asked hopefully. "You started to feel something for me, am I right?"

She nodded again. "Old Tiger needed you. He said you had information about agents in Latin America and South Florida that he needed. I didn't know what he was talking about until just now. But it's over - I mean, everything is different now. God, I've been so stupid." She sobbed softly and pressed towards him, but Eli shook her by the shoulders to bring her back into focus.

"Look, you've got me in a real box here. Don't fade out on me now. What was it you said about an old debt?"

"He said," she stammered, "that you killed one of his best men some years ago, and he wanted what you took from him." Eli racked his brain trying to think of whom the bastard could have been talking about, whom he could have been using before Eli retired in '84. Nothing came to him, and he was just about to continue with Mai Lee when Old Tiger yelled down at them from the bungalow deck.

"Come up to dinner, children, or do I need to send someone down to get you?"

Eli waved back in his general direction and pulled the girl along the trail. "You've got to stall for time," he whispered. "Tell him you need me to get you back into China. Tell him something, anything to buy me a little time so I can get us out of here." She nodded as they climbed the steps to the deck and walked into the refreshingly cool bungalow. The dinner table had been set with fine china and crystal and the food was overwhelmingly attractive to them.

"Please my dear, sit here." The old man took her hand and escorted her to one end of the teak table. "Mr.

Rose, you sit there in the middle where we can both talk to you." Mai Lee shivered and rubbed her arms with the sudden change in temperature, and her huge dark nipples stuck boldly to her damp shirt. "Perhaps you would like to change before dinner, my dear?"

"Yes, please," she said reticently.

"Ngyuen will show you to your room. We'll just have a drink while we wait." Mai Lee stood to leave and the old man bowed to acknowledge her departure. "Now Mr. Rose, may I pour you a glass of wine?" Eli nodded but said nothing. "It's a lesser Bordeaux I'm afraid, but all I can manage around here. My old French hosts would not have approved, but still it's not bad for my limited wine cellar."

"Cheers," Eli added, sipping the robust liquid. Mai Lee returned in a rush wearing a dry shirt and a bra, an unusually modest statement that made Eli think she feared for herself as well as for him. They ate rapidly but Eli took little notice of the food, other than he was finally able to satisfy his hunger. He listened to Old Tiger through dinner without commenting, trying to find some chink in the armor that might allow him to gain an advantage. Immediate action had to be ruled out, Eli decided, because of the two attentive armed guards that stood at either side of the table. Their gazes never shifted from him.

"Now, my dear," said the smooth old man as he stood, "Mr. Rose and I have some personal business to discuss."

"Eli............," she began.

"It's Ok. Maybe we can work out whatever problems we have here and come up with some type of amicable solution." Eli stared at her unconvincingly as the guards approached to escort her from the table.

"Yes, that's right. You see my dear, you have nothing to fear. I'm certain we can come to some mutually agreeable arrangement that satisfies both our needs." He smiled knowingly, and Eli was suddenly swept by a familiar sickening feeling. Old Tiger barked some rapid orders to the two guards and said, "These two gentlemen will escort you to your room, my dear. I will join you later to discuss the details our business."

They strode quickly up to Mai Lee and ushered her out the door as she looked back in panic. Eli hoped the old man planned to honor his deal with her uncle, but he suspected otherwise. Old Tiger turned his chiseled face toward Eli and now his expression was less welcoming. "You and I have much to discuss Mr. Rose. I think it best we do this in more appropriate surroundings. Please, stand up."

Another guard appeared at the door to encourage Eli to move, and as he approached Eli decided to make his move. The guard got too close and Eli pulled his Type 81 forward, throwing him off balance and directly into his upward-moving elbow. The blow caught him cleanly on the bridge of the nose and the guard groaned and dropped to the floor in a pool of blood. Eli ripped the rifle from his prostrate body and shoved it into Old Tiger's stomach. "Now, let's you and me take a little walk to see Miss Jones."

"How tiresome you are," the old man sighed. "If

you wish, but this is all so unnecessary." But he complied and turned and walked out the door with the Type 81 jammed into his back. They walked slowly across the square toward a small air conditioned guest house, and Eli felt certain he would be able to at least get a head start out of the compound before the guards caught on. The sound of running feet behind him caused his stomach to knot. A quick look over his shoulder confirmed the worst. A dozen of Old Tiger's men stood ready to shoot, their guns drawn and aimed at Eli from assorted distances.

"Take your pick my friend," the old man chuckled. "Any one of them is a crack shot and would be happy to oblige your suicidal tendencies in a second. All I need do is nod my head."

Eli grabbed Old Tiger by the collar and spun him around, using his body as a shield. That caused the group to rush quickly towards the pair to within a few short feet, so Eli brandished the rifle and pointed it at the old man's head menacingly. The men stopped in their tracks but Old Tiger just laughed. "So, you think this will help? This was your brilliant escape plan? Really, this is tiring."

"Shut up! Tell them to back off or I'll kill you right here."

"Really? So what will become of Miss Jones when you've done that? Shall I tell you? After you are quickly killed she will be passed around the compound for the men to enjoy. Then they will cut her into small pieces and feed her to the ants. I know you wouldn't want that, would you? Now, may I have the gun so we can conclude this embarrassing interruption?"

Eli knew he'd blown his chance. He'd already let slip his feelings for the girl and that gave Old Tiger all the leverage he needed. It was no use continuing, so he relaxed his grip on the old man's collar and lowered the gun. A group of Old Tiger's loyal guards jumped on Eli at once, twisting his arm behind his back until he fell to the ground in pain. "Take him to the exercise building," said Old Tiger, adjusting his shirt.

Eli fought like a wounded lion all the way to the dingy building, determined to make everything as difficult on them as possible. He even managed to kick loose for a second and smash one of the guys in the knee, sending him writhing to the ground. They swarmed on him and soon, all his voluntary movements were controlled. Eli noticed a large meat hook hanging from the center of the filthy room. It reminded him of some cheap horror movies he'd seen as a kid, that he now seemed to be part of. The lights were turned on and Eli's wrists were bound tightly with a small loop left open at the top of the wrapping. The loop was used to suspend him from the hook, which was just high enough to make his arms stretch but still keep his feet on the floor. "Mr. Rose, I am quite prepared to do this the hard way if necessary but I will start by asking you some simple questions. If I receive the answers I want, then I will be compassionate and may consider releasing you. If not, you will die a very painful death."

Old Tiger paced slowly in front of his prisoner while Eli's shirt was ripped off. Sweat streamed off him in lines and his head pounded with the surrealism of his predicament. "You know my friend, the mind does such strange things to the body when it perceives danger." He paused in the shadows long enough for Eli to notice a dull red glow suddenly materialize beside Old Tiger. "Nothing may be happening, yet the mind anticipates the pain and tries to prepare the body against it. Your mouth dries, your breathing becomes more rapid, you sweat, your pulse quickens."

The lights were abruptly turned out and Eli jumped at the drastic change. He could hear movement around him but could see nothing until the dull red glow flashed by, followed by blinding pain. The short hissing sound quickly subsided, leaving Eli in agony. The searing pain cut through his reasoning so fast he wasn't able to completely comprehend it. The shock of the metal against his ribs caused him to jerk convulsively against the bindings and Eli slumped dizzily as he fought to regain his senses. He gasped for breath and sweated violently. "What? What do you want?"

"A very good question," said the old bastard calmly. His voice was strangely soothing in the darkened room but Eli was hardly comforted. "Let's begin with the names of your key contacts in Central and South America and South Florida."

Eli laughed nervously, trying to relax himself as much as to throw the old guy a curve. "Look, you have to know I've been out of the business for years. I don't know anyone now."

"Oh come now, Mr. Rose. You had plenty of help eluding us in Costa Rica. Perhaps we need to refresh your memory a bit."

An instant later the pain reappeared, this time emanating from his back. "Stop!" Eli screamed. "I don't know anything. I don't............," and then it came again. Eli must have lost consciousness, because his next memory was a confused jumble of shouts and violent shakes. He was wet and aching and disoriented in the darkness.

"My poor friend," sighed Old Tiger from the blackness of the darkened room. "I know this is un-pleasant for you, but you see I am a very patient man. It's quite true that I need your information - it could make things so much easier for me. I am prepared to wait as long as necessary, so I suppose we must continue."

"Even if I knew something," Eli groaned, "the information would be worthless to you now. It's been so long."

"Perhaps - but we shall see. Again!"

"Wait," Eli stammered, searching for some way to stall him. "Mai Lee said you had some kind of debt to settle with me. Is that why you're doing this?"

"Oh, yes. Thank you so much for reminding me." The pain came again but only briefly. "Yes, I suppose I do owe you an explanation. After all, you killed one of my best operatives and stole something that was very valuable to me."

"Who?" Eli shouted at the blackness. "Who was it?

What did I take? I'll give it back, I swear it!" All he could think of was holding off the pain a little while longer, trying to regroup his strength for the next attack.

"I know you will recognize the name. He was a rather well-placed official of the Cuban government and a valuable man for me - Juan Pedraza."

"I don't know anyone named Pedraza," Eli lied, his heart pounding in his ears.

"Ah, but I know that you killed him. My information is very reliable." His voice changed inflection and became sharper, more direct. His passive interest had turned to active anger. "You cost me $1 million Mr. Rose and my distribution network in Miami. You see, Pedraza was the perfect front man. His position as a senior government official and his rather extensive network of Cuban agents was how I moved my cargoes from Cuba to Miami. It took a long time for me to set that up, and you ruined it all with your meddling. Now you can tell me the names of your contacts and who I need to speak with to gain access to Pedraza's network."

Old Tiger calmed a bit and there was a tinge of irony in his voice. "You know, he hadn't even paid me for that last shipment when you so inconveniently killed him. Castro refused to take my calls after that incident. Can you believe it? He blamed the whole thing on me. That little morality play of yours ruined a beautiful relationship, my friend."

"Look, you've got the wrong guy. Sure I was there, but I'm telling you, I didn't take the money and I don't know anything about Pedraza or his network."

"What a pity," he sighed. "Everyone, apparently we must have the wrong man." Eli heard muffled laughter from around the room. "Then as I mentioned, perhaps your memory will clear sufficiently for you to tell me who we should be speaking with."

The dull red glow seared into Eli's brain again, and everything was suddenly quiet.

Chapter 12

A strange sensation of weightlessness surrounded Eli, as if he was floating gently in space. He slowly began to realize that he actually was floating, or more precisely hanging, suspended three feet above the ground in a Vietnamese "Tiger Cage." His hands were free but badly cramped by the ropes that had bound him. The cage swayed slowly in the early morning breeze, and Eli smelled the distinct odor of rain in the air. He realized he must have lost consciousness one last time, and painfully assessed the damage to his aching body.

He had several small punctures and burns, but none were too serious - yet. The unfortunate reality was that there could soon be a continuation of the previous night's activities. He was convinced that an escape had to be made at all costs, since it was very probable he wouldn't survive another session in "The Exercise Building." Eli tried to focus on a plan; he had to regain some edge so that he could get out of the mess he was in. Exhaustion continued to pound and pull him under, and reality slipped away again.

Eli. Eli, wake up."

The voice whispered softly, like the wind rustling in the trees. He'd slept fitfully and came out of it feeling wretched and sodden. His body ached and stank of mud and sweat, and his thoughts were scrambled and disjointed. "How long have I been out?"

"Almost two hours. I had to watch you from distance to make sure you were awake before I came to help. You were screaming all night. It was horrible. Give me your hands." The girl produced a long switchblade from the back pocket of her trousers and began to cut through Eli's bindings. "Ok, I'm almost through. There," she said, and the bindings were suddenly loose.

Eli stripped them off his bloody wrists while Mai Lee unlatched the door to the cage. He jumped through the door and grabbed her arm in one motion, pulling her into the nearby brush. She fell on him and he winced in pain. During the previous evening he'd lost count of the number of times Old Tiger had tried to "persuade" him to talk with that hot iron bar, but now he could feel every one of the burns.

Mai Lee started to apologize for hurting him but Eli stifled her with his hand, shaking his head and imploring her to be quiet. He could hear the sound of boots in the jungle coming toward them, and he needed the element of surprise more than ever. She nodded her head and rolled off him to his right. Eli motioned for her to stay low while he gathered himself for what he had to do.

Eli could see the guard break the trees as he walked toward them. The guy paused briefly to light a cigarette and take a few puffs before he continued on the path back to the "Tiger Cage." Eli jumped him just before the guy could access the clearing. The guard had his Type 81 slung over his right should with one hand on the barrel, while the other held the cigarette. Eli grabbed the gun barrel and drove it sharply up and into the guy's nose. Stunned, the guard fell backwards and Eli pounced on top of his chest using his legs to pin the man, then slammed his left arm against the guy's windpipe to suffocate him. The blow was so strong that it crushed the guard's larynx instantly, so Eli was able to finish the job quickly and without any additional noise or disturbance.

He stripped the gun and ammunition belts from the prostrate form and then dragged the lifeless body into the dense underbrush just off the path. Eli quickly moved back to Mai Lee, who looked absolutely terrified but ready to follow him.

"Let's go, and stay close."

She nodded and they slipped off down the path until they could see the dormitories and guard house. "Stay here," he whispered and started off towards Old Tiger's bungalow.

"What are you doing?" said Mai Lee.

"I came for that statue and I'm going to leave with it, one way or the other."

"Are you crazy? We have to get out of here."

Eli glared at the girl and she froze. "I've been

through too much to leave here empty handed. China's that way if you want to go."

She shook her head so Eli continued on towards the bungalow, Mai Lee following.

Although the front entrance to the building sat on the open parade square, the rear door opened out to a much smaller clearing and the jungle beyond. He maneuvered around through the jungle to the back of the building and then ran up the back steps to the rear door. He found it unlocked, *a great example of overconfidence and carelessness*, he thought.

Eli entered the bungalow quietly and made straight for the dining room. He flipped the rifle around so it hung off his back and picked up the statue. Just as he turned to leave he saw Ngyuen enter the room from the kitchen. The servant didn't see the pair at first and began to walk across the room towards them. Eli gripped the statue with both arms and with a wide, baseball-style swing smacked Ngyuen in the side of the head as hard as he could

The impact made a sickening sound, like a raw egg makes when it's dropped onto a hard surface. Ngyuen crumpled to the floor without a sound. When Eli looked at the damage he also realized that the head of the statue had broken off. He stared for a second at Mai Lee but she rushed over and reached inside the body cavity, extracting a small cloth bag. She shoved the bag in her pocket and turned to leave.

"This is all we need," she whispered. Eli replaced the headless statue on its pedestal and they slipped out the back of the bungalow and into the jungle.

§

Eli pointed the direction they should go and he led the way. In order to move quietly they also had to move slowly, so after what seemed like an eternity they had slipped under the perimeter wire, completing a wide arc around the remaining camp facilities, and were headed north through the jungle.

"Listen," Eli whispered. "We have to go north towards China, get as far away from here as we can. Can you move fast?"

"I think so," she replied.

"Ok then," and he began to jog along the trail they had followed on their way into Vietnam from China.

The trail was initially downhill, so they were able to jog for about 10 minutes before Mai Lee grabbed his shirt and pulled. "I need a break," she gasped.

Eli was also breathing hard so he stopped and they slipped off the trail and down the hill to hide and recover. All they could do was suck air and look at each for what seemed like several minutes. He soon made the "thumbs up" gesture to the girl and she nodded, so they climbed back up the hill to the trail and continued their jog downhill for a few more minutes. The path then began to curve back up the hill and Eli knew they were on the climb out of the valley and towards the border.

The uphill slog quickly drained the energy from them as if it flowed out through an open tap on their ankles. Eli knew the guards would have discovered the bodies by now and that Old Tiger would have his entire force out looking for them. They needed to move swiftly, but that had become impossible in the stifling humidity. They were soaked with sweat and their clothes were ripped and covered in mud and leaves. They pushed on until Mai Lee suddenly collapsed in a heap.

Eli rushed back to her but she was unresponsive, so he grabbed her arms and pulled her onto his chest, then slid down the hill to look for water. He left the girl lying in the bushes and slipped and stumbled down the hill until he reached the bottom. As he guessed, a small stream flowed in the narrow valley, so Eli returned to Mai Lee and dragged her down to the cool water. He put her wrists into the stream to lower her body temperature and poured water over her face until her eyes opened.

"Where are we?" she asked.

"Maybe four miles from the border, more or less. Come on, drink here."

"But Eli, it's not clean."

"Yeah, I know. But we'll both die of heat stroke and dehydration if we don't drink now. We can suffer the consequences later, if we're still alive to worry about it."

Mai Lee didn't have to be asked twice, and she plunged her face into a clear, gentling flowing pool and drank until she'd had enough.

"I think we've got a good start on them and it will take them a while to figure out which way we've gone. We can rest here for a few minutes." He unstrapped the Type 81 and handed it to her. "Keep watch for a few minutes. I just need to stretch out my arms." Eli laid back against the leaf-covered slope of the hill and was asleep in an instant.

He awoke with a start, mad at himself for losing control in such a critical situation. *Wow, I'm really getting old*, he thought.

"Eli, I've been terrified the whole time you were asleep that they'd find us. Here, take this back." She handed him the dirty Type 81 like it was a dead animal she'd picked up off the road.

"How long was I asleep?"

"Less than an hour, but I'm really frightened."

"Ok. It's getting dark and that will give us some added cover, so let's get moving."

They walked slowly at first, stopping frequently to listen for anything out of the ordinary in the jungle's nighttime serenade. Eli wanted to stay off the main track now, since it was likely that Old Tiger's trackers would have found their trail. They roughed-it through the underbrush, following the general contours of the land back towards their potential salvation in China. He pulled the clip on the Type 81 and found it nearly full. It was the first time he'd thought to check it since they left. At least that was something positive.

They reached the crest of a low hill and Eli saw the distant lights of Ningming, China flickering to the north and Lộc Thanh, Vietnam just to their south. *We must be no more than 2 miles from the border*, he thought with relief. But which way to go? *Ningming is farther off, and Mai Lee might have contacts there we can use. But we can get to Lộc Thanh faster. Maybe Old Tiger has friends there? Not the best choice.*

Mai Lee flopped down against a large rock, and Eli settled in beside her desperately trying to clear his head so he could make the right choice. She gasped for breath and stared blankly at the tangled vines and grasses, as if expecting them to burst suddenly to life and imprison her.

Eli thought for a second as he crouched with the rifle. "Mai Lee, let's see the diamonds."

She slipped her hand into her dirty khaki pants and produced the small cloth bag. Eli took it from her carefully and untied the blue corded top with shaking hands. There they were, huge and plentiful, wrapped in white paper and flashing brilliantly in the moonlight like the stars over their heads. He folded them back up and handed her the bag. She put it back in her loose pants and shifted to her knees, ready to leave.

Before she could move another inch, Eli shoved the muzzle of the rifle into her smooth, flat stomach and pulled the bolt back into the ready position. She gulped a breath and held it, staring at him in disbelief. "Eli, what......?"

"I'm so sorry, babe," he whispered. "See, I just can't

trust you. The whole thing just doesn't make sense to me, and it never has. Everything that's happened, everything you said, it was all a lie." Eli put his finger on the trigger and looked at her intently. Tears were streaming down her face and all she could do was stare at him, wide-eyed.

"Eli, please don't."

"Please don't? Give me one good reason why I shouldn't? You and your friends have played me like a fool from the get-go. I haven't heard anything even remotely close to the truth since this whole thing started, and for all I know, you and that old bastard set up this escape just for his amusement. What's next, huh? You going to screw me so I'll tell him what he wants to know? Is that next? IS IT?"

"It's not true, it's not true!" she sobbed. "You've got to believe me, I didn't know about any of this. It wasn't my idea for this to happen." She cried quietly and moved to reach out for him but Eli forced her back with a sharp jab of the gun barrel. "I'm on your side. I love you, I couldn't hurt you."

The lack of sleep and food, the drugs, the torture all played havoc with Eli's senses and emotions. His stomach twisted in knots. His brain was a torrent of exhausted, conflicting thoughts. He stared at the pitiful girl crying in front of him. The outward projection of cold confidence Eli always wore like a cloak dropped away and he relented, putting his arms around her and hugging her tightly.

"It's Ok, it's Ok," he said quietly. "Alright, I believe you. I guess this didn't work out for you any better than it did for me, so now we're both caught up in this mess." She continued the sob and nod her head while he tried to comfort her, unaware that the night sounds of the jungle had suddenly changed.

"It's Ok, you can stop crying. Come on, you can give me the whole story when we're out of this godforsaken place and back in a cushy hotel in China. Deal?" He held her at arm's length, looking into her eyes.

Mai Lee looked up at him and began to smile, but was abruptly interrupted by the unmistakable thud of a bullet impacting against a tree just behind them.

"Down!" he yelled, pulling her to the ground beside him. Eli sniffed the air like a spooked deer and tried to get a sense of the distance and direction of the shot. "Must be some trackers out ahead of the main group. They'll try to circle and flank us if they can to show the big man how brave they were. Come on, we're not going to be here when they show up."

Mai Lee looked at him expectantly for a second so Eli waved at her to stay low and move back down the trail. As he slipped away a bullet smashed into the space behind her, shattering the rock into fine white powder. They scrambled clumsily but quickly on their hands and knees through the cutting, jagged underbrush. Sometimes they crouched and ran a short distance and other times they crawled like blind crabs though the blacked out jungle.

Another 50 yards or so and we'll run for it, Eli thought. *Ten. Twenty. Forty. There, now we go.* He signaled Mai Lee to follow him and they began a headlong dash through the vines and razor grass, bouncing off trees and tripping on fallen logs. The feeling of panic quickly became palpable for each of them as they ran, and it drove them forward like terrified animals. It felt like their pursuers were just behind them, almost touching their backs or ready to bring them down with a bullet in another second. They could almost *feel* those monsters breathing down their necks.

They were being cut to ribbons by the razor-sharp blades but continued headlong down the trail. Eli panted and heaved trying to catch his breath. The hair on the back of his neck bristled like the hair of a rabid dog. He *knew* they were out there, even if he couldn't hear them. He could *feel* it. They kept running, and Eli shoved Mai Lee past him so that he didn't lose her in the blackness. She stumbled and Eli spun forwards over her and down a small slope. He instantly realized he'd fallen back into the small stream.

Eli reached up and grabbed Mai Lee by her long legs and yanked her down the slope on top of him, covering her mouth with his grimy hand. "Do you have the knife you used to cut me loose?" She slowly pulled the large switchblade from her rear pocket. Eli grabbed it and sprung the blade open, tucking it in against his chest to keep it from reflecting the moonlight like a beacon. They waited in the muddy meander for what seemed like an eternity, listening for the tell-tale crack of a twig or brush of a branch to signal the location of the approaching patrol. Finally, the pop of a breaking branch caught Eli's attention; then another, and another, and then very close above him, the sound of controlled breathing.

Voices suddenly materialized out of the background chatter of birds and insects, maybe 10 yards or so to Eli's left. Three or four guys, quietly discussing the situation between themselves in Vietnamese. A minute or so passed and they wandered off down the main trail, the sound of their boots on the dirt fading with Eli's fear. He relaxed slowly and was about to start moving again when the bushes just above rustled and shook, and one of the soldiers slid down onto the bank only three feet away. The guy paused in a crouch for a few seconds, ready for the unknown and listening for some sign of the escapees.

Eli and Mai Lee held their breath as the guy moved slowly down the stream bed to their right, passing directly in front of them. Eli tightened his grip on the knife handle as the soldier inched by and jumped from his covered refuge, catching the guy from behind. Eli reached around him in one fluid motion, as he had been taught to do so many years before, and pulled the guy's chin towards the sky with his left hand. In the same motion, he brought the razor-edged blade across the guy's carotid artery with his right hand, swiftly digging in and ripping out towards the jungle. The knife did its job with lethal efficiency and the poor sod dropped his rifle and fell limply to his knees, gurgling great geysers of blood into the once crystal clear water. He dropped face first into the stream bed without another sound. Eli quickly rifled the dead soldier's pack for his extra ammo clips and hopped back into the shadows with Mai Lee.

"Here," he said, handing her the dripping blade. "Thanks for the loan. Now let's move." She winced and wiped it off on her pants. They slowly made their way past the corpse, trying not to slip on his blood as it mingled with the cool water, and followed its trail downstream towards their hoped-for salvation.

Chapter 13

"Just a little farther, then we'll rest." China was the call, since Eli felt there would be too much risk of alerting Old Tiger if they tried to contact the authorities in Lộc Thanh. So the ragged pair followed the lower contours of the hills as the early morning darkness drained away to dawn. They crouched and crawled, slinking through the thorns and gripping the vines like monkeys. There had been no sign of Old Tiger's men since their encounter in the stream, so the two escapees moved faster and also noisier than before. Eli wanted to cross into China by first light but soon realized that they would still be too close to Vietnam. "Close" only counts in horseshoes, so they say, and that wasn't quite good enough for him.

"Eli, I've got to stop," whispered Mai Lee hoarsely. She dropped down beside a large tree, a pitiful site for his tired eyes considering her formerly regal beauty.

"Ok - Wait here while I scout ahead a little farther." She nodded faintly and Eli continued on, past a hilltop and into a small clearing in just a few steps. *This is it,* he thought. Finally, the lights of Ningming lay in the valley below them, a couple of miles to their north. They'd had made it back to The People's Republic; now, hopefully, Mai Lee's numerous connections could save them.

Eli trotted back to the spot where he'd left her, draped against the tree like a Salvador Dali clock, and was stopped in his tracks; she was gone! Instinctively, the ex-commando fell into a crouch and listened, trying to hear and see some sign of his employer through the tangled ground cover. The first dim light of a new day crept carelessly towards him, caressing the hills and illuminating the shadows. Eli suddenly saw Mai Lee's frightened face under the branches of a large bush, and she waved at him to come to her. He scrambled through the thicket as fast as he could because he knew that if he could see her, someone else might easily have seen him. Just as Eli slipped in next to her, the drone of a helicopter engine erupted through the background of waking birds and terrified monkeys. Mai Lee gestured over towards the hilltop Eli had just come from, where Highway S325 to Ningming passes smoothly along the border. He looked back and saw them - the old man's Hind gunships hovering just above the trees.

"Come," Eli whispered, sliding around through the thick, damp leaf mat and finally down the hill. They slipped into a small valley, really a crevasse and began to weave their way down the hill away from the border. The newly planted rice fields beckoned to them like a friendly wet lawn but they dared not enter because of the grievous lack of cover.

"What do we do now?" whispered the girl. She sensed Eli's alarm at the last 50 yards and stared at him expectantly, waiting for some miraculous act to spring forth from his soggy brain.

"Wait a second," Eli said, trying desperately to grasp the scene. He was overcome by a sudden flash of *déjà vu*, realizing he'd seen this picture once before. It sent a chill up his spine. "I smell a major trap in the making."

As if on cue from some great celestial play, a line of 50 or 60 men spontaneously appeared in the field ahead, guns pointed in their direction. The men were spread out before the two escapees like a beater line in a tiger hunt and Eli fought to stifle a laugh at the Tiger's ingenuity. He readied the little gun as they advanced but knew that the outlook was not promising. "Mai Lee, I want you to move to my right about 50 feet, and when I start firing I want you to run like hell."

"No," she said flatly. "Sorry, I just can't manage that without you." Eli glared into her bloodshot eyes but quickly realized there was no way short of carrying her that she'd follow that order. He shook his head and crouched for cover behind a craggy piece of gray limestone that would also likely serve as their tombstone.

"Mr. Rose, Miss Jones, please come out now. The game is over." The strangely calm and comforting voice blared at them through a loudspeaker. Old Tiger's helicopter faced them as if he knew they were waiting for him to arrive. "Now, now, children. We have you surrounded. We know exactly where you are. Please come out with your hands raised over your heads so that we can all go home quietly, without any further bloodshed. Miss Jones, I must insist that you show yourself now. I do not wish to have to explain to your uncle how you came to grief here."

"Well, boss," said Eli to the dark-haired angel, "that's your chance. You can beat it out of here and he'll probably send you safely back to your uncle. Seems like he needs him as an ally and fears him as an enemy."

"Not a chance," she smiled faintly.

"If that's your answer then I'm sorry to say that this looks like the end of the road for both of us. Sorry I screwed it up for you."

"No, don't say that," she cried. "It was a wonderful ride, it really was." Mai Lee smiled through her tears and hugged Eli's arm.

"Ok then. We don't have much of a chance, so let me tell you how it will go. They'll come in a few at a time, mainly from the flanks. When they first start moving within range, I want you to keep your head low and stay down until I tell you to move. Got it?"

"Got it, boss," she smiled thinly.

"Right." Eli flashed a confident smile, knowing it was a lie. Whether he could trust her or not, they had both fallen into the same boat in the end, and now it was sinking with both of them in it. Regardless of her motives, she was staring at the guns just like Eli was. He crouched stiffly, like an over-wound spring ready to explode, consciously restraining the urge to fire until he could see the fillings in their teeth.

"Down - now!" Eli said, and he sprang forward with the rifle blazing. He focused his first burst on the left flank, and sprayed the outside 10 men in three rapid sweeps. They screamed and toppled backwards at awkward angles as the 7.62 millimeter rounds ripped through their limbs and bodies. The others instantly returned fire and dropped behind a low levee for cover. His ruse had given them a minute and brief chance off to the right. Smashing at their *right* flank was meant to make them overcompensate to Eli's *left*, drawing their pursuer's interest and concentrating their fire in the wrong place. Bullets whizzed randomly around Eli and Mai Lee as the soldiers blasted every rock and tree they could see. Eli tapped Mai Lee on the back and motioned for her to begin to slide over to the right, to temporary haven behind another large boulder.

The helicopters fired off short spreads of rockets that landed well up the hill behind them, yet the explosions shook their internal organs violently and cracked their eardrums. Eli could see through the haze of cordite that Old Tiger's men had begun their advance, now in standard two-by-two cover, and the right flank would be tougher than he'd thought. Just as he was about to begin a last pass at the road, one of the men farthest in front exploded in a muddy red cloud of water and body parts. "Mine field!" Eli shouted. "They hit a damned mine field! Must be a left-over of the '79 war." But the soldiers didn't freeze the way Eli thought they would. They whirled around instead and had begun shooting crazily away from the pair and back *towards* China. Eli gingerly stuck his head out to look at the mass hallucination and started to laugh.

"What?" asked the girl, thinking he'd lost his mind. "What is it?"

"It's not a mine field," laughed Eli. "It's the goddamn People's Liberation Army, coming up the highway like the frigging U.S. cavalry. Can you believe it! We're being rescued by these assholes and they don't even know it!"

Eli fell backward against the rock, nearly hysterical with relief. The exhausted pair watched as a large armored infantry unit inched its way up the road under a barrage of withering fire from the gunships hovering up the hill above them. The Chinese scattered into a disorganized charge, firing wildly as they advanced through the smoke and dust. Suddenly, the helicopters broke off their lethal rain of cannon fire and pivoted around, flying quickly southwest up the valley and back into Vietnam. Eli was cheered at their retreat, only to see them reappear on the other side of the hill firing missiles into the column from the left rear flank. One of the Chinese T-72M tanks erupted into a muffled ball of orange flame as the Hinds shifted their attention back to the exposed infantry. Though he hated the notion of being rescued by the PLA, they were the most likely salvation available, and they were being cut to ribbons in front of him. Eli maneuvered down to the base of the hill and set up his position for crossfire.

"Damn it guys," he said aloud. "Take the stupid

gunships out already." Eli raised his rifle and prepared to shoot at them himself but was preempted by an ear-splitting roar. The deafening sound fractured the entire scene, temporarily stunning the foot soldiers on both sides and briefly halting the hostilities. Even the weapons officers on board the choppers seemed to freeze momentarily as a pair of Chinese J-8II's screamed over the valley at tree-top level. As soon as they had surveyed the situation they peeled off in opposite directions and flashed off down the valley to turn.

"They're from the base at Nanning," Eli yelled through the din. "They must have been asleep or something."

The jets wheeled around to launch their first attack run and the Hinds instantly scattered up the hill in a vain attempt to stay low. The fighting in the field had resumed but Eli resisted the urge to lash out at Old Tiger's men and just stayed quiet, watching the developing dogfight overhead. Three of the choppers see-sawed through the trees, trying to slip through the narrow pass at the back of the valley while the other two made a dead run straight up the hill. The two J-8II's shot in from the northeast and made straight for the last two Hinds, launching SRAAM missiles at almost point-blank range. Eli could actually see one of the missiles hit the front nacelle of the lead Hind, disintegrating the rotor and tail section and sending the smoldering hulk spinning into the jungle.

A cheer erupted from the Chinese on the road and their firing increased by an order of magnitude. The other helicopter tried to pirouette back down the hill but was tagged by another SRAMM dead-on the main rotor, crashing in a heap in the rice paddy below. The other three "dragon flies" had managed to make the mountain pass by staying in the trees, which Eli guessed might have prevented the J-8II's from getting a radar lock for their missiles. Their good fortune was short-lived, however, when the fighters let loose with their 30 mm cannons at close range. All three of the ugly gunships were ablaze as they pounded into the dense jungle floor.

The dogfight preoccupied the Chinese pilots for several minutes but they still had enough presence of mind to return to the fray on the ground after their lopsided victories. The land battle had continued unabated on the field in front of Eli and Mai Lee, and the PLA had progressively ripped into Old Tiger's troops with horrific results. The jets raked the ground with their 30 mm guns and sent the rabble that was once a tightly woven paramilitary force fleeing back towards the border. The only problem with that was that Eli and Mai Lee sat between them and their salvation. The PLA troops, freshly inspired by their airforce's quick work of the helicopters, charged up the valley in hot pursuit of Old Tiger's men. A hand-to-hand melee ensued with Old Tiger's survivors, and the well-ordered battle lines quickly dissolved around the stranded couple.

"Eli!" screamed Mai Lee. Eli looked to his right just in time to see the first of Old Tiger's men break cover to get an exposed shot at them. The little Type 81 chattered away as if it had a mind of its own, throwing Eli off balance back against the rock. He jerked the gun up involuntarily and caught the lead guy completely by luck, full in the chest as he dashed in. The killer round caught him on the bridge of the nose, bursting his head like an over-ripe melon. "Watch out!" she screamed again, and suddenly the firefight was all around them. The Chinese had managed to chase the remnants of the drug lord's army right into their position, and soon Eli was deep into the fight. "There - There! Two in front!"

"I know, I know!"

"Three there, to the right!"

"Yeah! Yeah!"

"Yow!" she yelled. Eli whirled around just a second too late to catch the guy that jumped out of the bushes above them. It didn't look like he expected Eli to be there either, since he never had a chance to get a shot off before they collided. The guy landed on Eli with full force, knocking the Type 81 to the ground. Eli rolled immediately, trying to throw him off, but the guy suddenly became limp and dropped to the ground. Mai Lee stood there holding her nasty little knife, but thanks would have to wait. They looked at each other, speechless for a moment and then Eli grabbed an extra clip, rammed it into the magazine and continued to fire into the jungle. The little gun got so hot that he had to rip the last few tatters of his shirt to shreds and wrap the pieces around the barrel.

"Hurry! Hurry!" she shouted through the din.

"Got him!"

"Two more - There, there!"

"I can't.......... Ok, it's cool. Look out!" Eli jerked her away from their comfy old rock just as two guys cleared the underbrush and fired, wildly spraying their hideout. Before Eli could get a shot off in return they both crumpled and fell backwards, dead. "Must be the Chinese," Eli said loudly. The sound of small arms fire began to drift away up the hill, and the fighting in the rice paddy quickly tapered off to silence. Eli thought better of their exposed position so they slid back into a small group of thorny bushes to watch the end of the fighting. The PLA regulars chased down the last fleeing stragglers of Old Tiger's well-oiled machine and methodically shot each of them.

Mai Lee reached up and pulled Eli close to her, and whispered, "Eli, they can't find me here."

"Why not? They're "friendlies" aren't they?"

"Not to me. Just trust me, they can't find me here. I have to go now."

"Go? Go where?" Eli asked, stunned at the thought.

"Never mind that. Just don't worry; I have some friends near here that can help me." Eli must have had quite a shocked look on his face because she continued to try to explain her departure. "Listen to me - Above everything else you might think, I want you to remember that I love you. I will always love you, no matter what happens. You'll be Ok without me now. Start speaking English right away. Tell them you're an

American and they'll think twice about shooting you. They'll take you to Beijing for questioning but I'm certain they'll eventually turn you over to the US embassy. I'm sorry but I've got to go now." Eli bent down and kissed her softly but quickly, and at the same time he felt he'd never see her again. The girl smiled sadly for a brief moment and then slid into the rice paddy, quickly disappearing behind the bushes.

The gunfire had completely stopped by then, and Eli saw the Chinese soldiers begin to search the jungle above him, talking loudly as they jabbed their bayonets into the prostrate bodies of their dead adversaries. Eli shoved the trusty Type 81 into the thorns behind him and struggled to his feet.

He was so tired, he could barely stand and he must have looked like a drunken idiot to the small group of men he approached. "Hey, comrades," Eli said hoarsely, his arms raised towards the humid morning sky, "American. I'm an American. Which way to the tourist information office? I've got some complaints about the noise around here."

Chapter 14

"Mr. Rose," said Richards again in measured tones, "why don't ya' just humor me one more time. See, ahm old and a bit hard a hearin.' In Texas we don't all speak as fast as you Yankees do, so I want ya' ta' give it to me real slow this time. Oh, and besides, ah don't concentrate as well as ah used ta' so ah need ya' ta' refresh ma' memory one more time if ya' please."

"Ok, fine Agent Fritz, or Fred, or whatever your *real* name is."

"It's Richards," said the agent. "That's ma' real name; Richards."

"Whatever," Eli said. "Ok, Agent *Richards*, last time this century I'm going to repeat this so listen up. It's like I told you - I was just doing a job. That's all, just a job."

"Doin' a job?" the agent crowed sarcastically. Hank Richards finally began heating up around the collar and he paced his well-appointed office more and more nervously by the minute. "Doin' a job? Ah'll give ya' a fuckin' job, jerkweed. A job is gettin' the State Department ta' pull enough strings down the street here ta' keep these bastards from fryin' ya' ugly little ass right now. Doin' a job is tryin' ta' convince these suspicious shits that we weren't behind that little party a yours in the first place. Ah'll tell ya' where ya' can put ya' job! Washington is madder than a nest fulla' yeller jackets. They think ya' were workin' some kind a clandes-tine thing out there fuh' *me*. Boy, ya' oughta' drop down on ya' knees and thank the good Lord above that this is a communist country, 'cause otherwise the press woulda' had a field day with ya' ass and ah couldn't a saved ya'. They'd a roasted ya' lame ass and ma' nuts in an open fire 'till the cows came home. Shee-it!"

His slow Texas twang did little to hide the anger of having been caught so off guard by the events in Ningming. He'd been caught with his pants down, peeing in the wind when the Chinese filed their formal complaint with Washington. "Shee-it!" he repeated slowly. "Those bastards didn't even give us the courtesy a hearin' about it first. They sent their fuckin' ambassador straight ta' the goddamn White House! Can ya' believe that! And oh man, didn't *that* just make the President's day!"

"Well, pass on my apologies to the President," Eli replied, "but it wasn't my idea to start World War Three and a Half out there."

"So whose fuckin' idea was it, smartass? Shee-it, just forget it. Ya' in so much hot wahta' it really don't matter who did what. But ah've got ta' go through this bullshee-it interview one more time fuh our Miss Davis here so that ma' pension doesn't take a fuckin' hike with the rest a ma' goddamn career!" Richards stomped off into the corner and lit a huge Cuban *Cohiba Siglo VI* cigar, which he inhaled emotionally.

"Ok, let's just say that ya' wanna' be a real nice guy and humor me. Maybe if ya' real nice, we can cut a 100 or 200 years off ya' prison term!" The lovely Miss Davis, his curvaceous blond stenographer, smiled weakly and sat with fingers poised to record Eli's every word. Richards, if that was really his name, sat down and propped his ostrich-skin ropers up on the corner of his massive teak desk and sucked hard on the huge brown cigar. "Go on, comrade," he grinned. "Do it 'till it hurts."

Grudgingly, Eli recounted as much of the story as he could, leaving out some of the key names of people he wanted to protect. As for the purpose of his "visit" and the results, Eli told him basically everything, or enough to make it all ring true. "Oh by the way, nice boots you have there," Eli added sarcastically.

"Pointy-toed boots ah fuh fairies, boy, and don't try ta' smoke me. Now cut the shee-it and let's have some answers." Miss Davis snickered quietly, causing Richards to grunt in disapproval. "Now ya' never said who hired ya' ta' do all this "Rambo" crap."

"That's because I never met the man," Eli lied. "I told you, all the contacts were by telephone or via a note delivered anonymously. I never saw anybody."

"Bullshee-it!" Richards sneered. "Horse hockey. Dammit, boy, ya' got more lie's than a house fulla'

French whores. Go on and finish this fantasy so we can get on with our lives."

"After I turned myself in to the Chinese, things were a little tense for a while."

"Well screw me! Ya' don't say? So what'd *they* do?"

Eli sighed loudly, ready to go back to the Chinese prison. "Ok. First stop was Nanning Regional Military Headquarters for interrogation. They were nice enough to keep me looking pretty for the secret police. I got the standard five w's + h - who, what, where, when, why, and how, kind of like this but at least they had enough brains to stop after the second day. Then they started with the psychological games, and that crap went on for a few days. When they were satisfied that I wasn't some hired man from Old Tiger's outfit they let the secret guys take me off to a lovely little cottage in the country."

"Where ya' told 'em..........."

"Where I told them the same shit I've been telling *all* of you guys for the past month." Eli lost his temper again. "You know, it never ceases to amaze me just how thick-headed all you government range riders are. You all ask the same stupid questions so many times, trying to trap people into to saying something conflicting. You're so transparent! Just a bunch of brain dead government zombies!"

Miss Davis stopped transcribing his comments, anticipating some kind of venomous outburst from her boss, but none came. Instead, he laughed and said, "Hell, yeah we're brain dead. Of course we ah. Who wouldn't be, havin' to sit here and listen ta' this fairy tale hour afta' hour? Ya' macho bastards ah all alike. God how I hoped "The Agency" woulda' rounded all ya' old dinosaurs up and sunk ya' at the bottom uh some fuckin' mine shaft." The pretty blond broke in abruptly and asked to excuse herself for a few minutes. "Sure honey, go ahead. We ain't gonna' be here much longer anyway." The two men stared diligently at her firmly rounded rear as she exited the room, and Richards said quietly, "God put her here ta' punish me. She's drivin' me nuts. Only decent piece ah ass fuh a thousand miles, and she won't even say 'boo' ta' me."

"Too bad," Eli chuckled. "You could always pork some old-hag diplomat's wife."

The burly Texan snarled through his cigar and smashed it carelessly into his ashtray. "Since ya' talkin' about pork, ya' might as well know that we're gonna' do this 'till ya' squeal like a stuck pig, boy, so stop bein' cute. And don't even try ta' ask me bout' my cee-gar. A smartass like ya' self probably already noticed it was Cuban, but that's just tough shee-it. The things ah legal over here, and this is fuckin' Red China - If ah can't get any decent pussy in this godforsaken country then at least ah damn sure can have a good cee-gar!"

"Three weeks in solitary," Eli continued drearily. "Sleep deprivation, sodium pentothal, you name it. Maybe they pulled something out that I'd forgotten or thought insignificant; I don't know. They didn't seem too upset with me after the third week, but that may have been because of Washington. Anyway, the last week of my stay they just left me in a small room with a guard on the door. They fed me regularly and let me piss in a bathroom for a change. That's about it."

"Yeah, that was it 'till ah got ma' hands on ya'. Nothin' more ta' say? Don't wanna' change anythin'? Still have the same story?" Richards looked at his crushed cigar and twirled it around in his stubby fingers.

"Same story," Eli said, trying to rub the kinks out of his stiff neck.

The girl slipped back into the room but Richards stopped her before she could sit down. "Miss Davis, that'll be all fuh now. I'll be sure ta' call ya' if ah need ya'. Thanks very much." She smiled at him, picked up her notes, and slipped back out of the room like a soft breeze.

"It's *Cinnamon Spice*," said Richards abruptly, catching Eli by surprise.

"What? What is?"

"*Cinnamon Spice* - It's her perfume, goddammit! Don't ya' know shee-it? It's the hottest thing state-side. Drives me fuckin' loco!"

"Sorry. I've been away for awhile," Eli sighed. "Look, Richards, "I've given you everything you asked for. How about answering a couple of questions for me for a change?"

He stood up suddenly and threw the battered cigar to the floor with a flourish. The clean-cut old Texas farm boy walked behind Eli slowly and tapped his shoulder lightly with his hand. "Friend, ah don't know if ya' noticed lately, but ya' ain't in any position ta' ask fuh anythin'."

Richards was so much a part of the rigging Eli fought to be free of years before, that stifling tangle of deceit and rigid conformity that permeated "The Agency" while he was there. Eli thought he'd managed to escape it all in Costa Rica but he should have known it would catch up to him sooner or later. The mere presence of the man made his hair bristle, even while he confessed to himself a slight admiration for Richards' no nonsense style. The bulky man stayed where he was, out of sight but very much a presence in the room. "Since ahm such a nice guy," he continued, "Ahm gonna' let ya' just fire away. If ah don't like the question, ah'll just ignore it."

"Fair enough," Eli said. He didn't like Richards, but he was becoming familiar to Eli and hopefully, predictable. "I never heard from the Chinese how things turned out with Old Tiger. Did they get him?"

"Yeah.............. When we heard what was goin' on down there, the group here took bets as ta' whether the Chinese would finally get the little snake ah not. From what ah've been able ta' piece together, they popped him pretty good. Laid waste ta' his camp and his whole operation, but they never found a body. About the time they decided ta' go lookin' fuh his head, the Vietnamese got a little bent outta' shape about them bein' on the wrong side a the border and really let 'em have it. Ya' great heroes had ta' beat it outta' there max quick."

"So what happened to him?"

"Ya' guess is as good as mine, son. He could be anywhere from Hanoi ta' Honolulu by now. Ya' have ta' ask ya' friends about that when they get here."

"My friends?"

"Well, we got a couple a real tough *hombres* comin' out ta' see ya' from Langley. Should be here tomorrow. That don't happen too often around these parts, so they must want ya' pretty damn bad." Eli could just imagine what was in store for him, and he would have almost rather been back with the Chinese. "See, ah figure ya' must be a real important guy ta' rate this, or ya' did somethin' even more stupid before ah got hold a ya'." He grinned like a Great White shark with a mouth full of gleaming, perfectly capped teeth. "Maybe ya' just a real bad *hombre*." Richards pushed the buzzer on his desk and asked his secretary to send the guard back into the room. "Relax while ya' can, boy. Ah'll let ya' know when the nut crushers get here."

The young Marine came in and stood rigidly at Eli's chair, waiting for him to leave, so he got up without saying another word, exiting the office swiftly. The Marine escorted Eli silently back to his Spartan quarters and locked him in for the night. The week he'd spent under house arrest at the embassy had provided many opportunities to think about his situation in life and as a result, Eli was depressed much of the time. He sat down heavily on his flimsy little bed and tried again to sort through the month-old magazines and newspapers he now cherished like gold. But they held little of interest for him after so long, and his thoughts drifted back to

Mai Lee and that last glimpse of her in the field. The image depressed him as usual, and he felt strangely lost, even though he knew she was free. If she'd been caught, Eli reasoned, either the Chinese or Americans would have let it slip by now, would have questioned him about her. He was somewhat cheered by the thought of her sleek form dressed to kill in Hong Kong, running the company she'd worked so hard to help build. Eli was sure to be a distant memory for her by now.

§

"Well, well, it's been a long time, hasn't it?" The extended boney hand belonged to Ahmed Djabouli. He grinned from ear to ear in that slimy way he always did. The last time Eli had had the pleasure, Djabouli wasn't quite as thrilled to see him.

"Ahmed," Eli said, shaking his hand limply. "So what rock did you crawl out from under this time?"

Djabouli laughed in his usual, high-pitched nasal way and shook his freakishly long index finger at Eli. "Ah, always the kidder. That was what I always liked about you, Rose." He turned to his plain-looking hulk of a companion and added, "He's a real good one for the jokes. Now to business - Sit down my friend. We have much lost time to cover."

Eli sat in Richards' chair and thrust his feet up onto the desk, taunting him with his lack of respect for the Station Chief's presence. Djabouli handed Eli a rum and soda, and Eli smiled at Richards, who was clearly agitated. "So Ahmed, what brings you all the way from Langley with your eunuch friend here? Surely you didn't come all the way out here just to see poor little insignificant me?"

The skinny Arab brushed his thick black hair to one side and leaned forward, as if to add emphasis to what he was about to say. It always seemed like a phony gesture of familiarity that Eli never shared. "You have made some very important people very angry with you, Eli. You should have had the good sense not to turn up in this way."

"You mean, it would have been better if I'd turned up dead?"

"Let's just say, you really could have picked a better time." He laughed to himself and continued, "You should have seen Morgan's face when he got the call from the Secretary of State. Bless Allah, but he was as mad as the fires of Hades. His face was twisted like one of those Cuban *pasteles* you used to eat, and he was screaming so loud I thought they would hear him on Pennsylvania Avenue."

"I wish I could have seen that," Eli said contritely. He knew that he should have stayed dead to "The Agency," *off the grid* as they called it. There would be a steep price to pay for showing up again suddenly and in such a publically embarrassing way.

Djabouli laughed again and tapped his silent friend on the shoulder. The big, square-jawed guy sat stiff as a stone and showed little emotion. He reminded Eli of a few ex-Navy SEALS he'd known during the war. "Did you hear what he said, Quentin? What a sense of humor you have, Eli. Really. But we must get down to business and stop wasting Mr. Richards' precious time. Now I want you to tell me the story once again, from the very beginning, leaving nothing out."

Richards smiled, sensing Eli's reaction. "Lick me, Ahmed," said Eli, sipping the drink.

The huge silent hulk, Quentin, suddenly stood bolt-upright like a broken spring and made a quick move towards Eli that looked like trouble. "It is Ok, Quentin," said Djabouli just quickly enough to prevent a sure beating. "That's just his way. Eli, maybe I should explain why Quentin was sent with me."

Eli waved his approval. "You see, Morgan remembered the last time he asked you to come in and what you did to the escort. That's why Quentin is here. He will be, ah, your personal escort until we return."

"I don't need an escort because I'm not going back with you."

Djabouli's black eyes flickered with anger, but he projected only a minor sign of displeasure. "You know, Rose, that I considered this job an insult."

"I could have guessed as much."

"It is a disgrace for me to have to deal with a man like you. You never offered anything to "The Agency." You were never loyal, nor did you ever prove to be much of an asset. I can't understand why Morgan likes you so much. The fact that I have to deal with you at all dirties me.................The son of a Jew............."

Eli slammed the glass down on Richards' desk, grabbed his letter opener, and jumped the desk in a second. He jammed the sharp instrument to within a millimeter of the olive-colored skin of Djabouli's neck. Quentin hopped up and started to grab for Eli, but Djabouli waved him off again, this time much less casually. "No, no, Quentin. It is Ok. He is not serious. He knows that I meant no offense, don't you Eli?"

"I do?" Eli growled. "You just insulted my family, Ahmed, and you know how mad I got the last time someone did that." Eli pushed the dull blade closer, until it had made contact with the Arab's neck. Djabouli smiled weakly and began to sweat. "Now be a good boy and say you're sorry, and don't say it in Arabic. Otherwise, I'll have to make a mess of Mr. Richards' nice Oriental rug, and I might just ruin your day all to hell, too."

"Yes, yes, I'm very sorry you were offended," he chuckled nervously. "I was only trying to get you to wake up and talk to us."

"That's better," Eli said, flipping the little blade towards Richards. He nearly collapsed trying to avoid the thing, which imbedded itself in the bookcase next to his head. "Shouldn't keep such dangerous things lying around in the open like that. Someone could have been hurt."

"Shee-it!" Richards yelled. "Would ya' pansies get on with this, or do ah have ta' call in the "Jar-heads" and have the lot ah ya' dumped in Outer Mongolia?"

"No, don't worry," shouted Djabouli. "No need to call the guards. I think we can continue our discussion without further difficulties. What do you think, Eli?"

"Sure, why not? Ok, one last time for you Ahmed,

but I'm only doing this because I like you so much." Eli smiled. The story ran like a tired old movie one more nauseating time, and Eli continued to leave out the pertinent details when necessary. He knew Djabouli would pick up on the things that Richards had missed, but he had no intention of telling him any more than Eli had told his older cohort.

"A very interesting story," said Djabouli. "May I ask you a few questions?"

"Oh, this oughta' be real cute," Richards chimed in with a smile.

"Sure, but I might choose not to answer them," Eli replied casually.

"That's fair. Let's start with your contact in Costa Rica."

"What contact?"

"Oh, come now, you certainly do have one. Even you would not have been able to pull off that escape without help."

"What escape?"

"Hah! Ya' see what ah mean? Let's fry the bastard right here," interrupted Richards, raising up from his chair with growing agitation.

"Eli, you're not being very cooperative." Djabouli began to pace in front of Eli with his hands clasped behind his back. "You don't expect me to believe that you planned and executed your escape without any local help, do you?"

"Why not?" Eli sneered. "I'm a pretty resourceful guy, remember?"

"Yes, you *were* once, a long time ago. But now you

are a drunken, washed up wreck of a man and I don't believe you can do much of anything these days except create trouble for us." Djabouli shook his head and frowned. "Alright then, let's try something different. Which side do you think your friend Mai Lee Jones is playing for?"

"Her own side," Eli added cynically, trying not to convey the surprise he experienced at having her name suddenly burst out.

"Oh Rose, be serious for a moment! Do you think she is a PRC agent or with the Taipei nationalists?"

"I just told you, she was in it for herself." Richards' shocked stare reinforced Eli's opinion that he could still keep some of the truth hidden, if only temporarily. "What makes you think she is either of those?" Eli asked, genuinely interested in the answer.

He'd hoped Djabouli would tell him something in the arrogant way he used to, flaunting his command of the facts to make himself feel smarter. This time, however, he kept his sources close. "Glory is to Allah but you're a pain in my ass. We are getting nowhere with this." The gaunt little Arab opened his briefcase and rummaged around for something while Richards strutted around the room like a mad rooster.

"Ah told ya' this guy was an asshole. Let's shee-it can the SOB and be done with it," Richards blurted out.

"Shut up you foolish man!" shouted Djabouli. He glared at Richards, who abruptly sat down in a huff. The Arab produced a small folder from the briefcase that contained a passport and an airline ticket, held them up for Eli to see and said, "You will be going back through Hong Kong with us tomorrow morning, on our way to Virginia. Should you have a change of heart and wish to introduce us to your friend, Miss Jones, we would be most grateful."

Eli glanced up at him quickly, wishing he hadn't been so quick to give up the letter opener. "Not a chance in hell."

"Fine. I had hoped it would not be necessary to transport you all the way back, but I see now that I was overly optimistic. Perhaps you will be more cooperative at "The Ranch."

Eli stood up and stretched the kinks out of his stiff back, and walked up to Richards, who now sat by impassively, picking at one of his cigars. "We'll see. Anyway, I was getting pretty sick of this place, I can tell you."

"The feelin's mutual, boy," said the older man with tired resignation. "We'll all be real sorry ta' see ya' go." He got up and walked over to the door, waving at Djabouli and pointing his finger in Eli's face. "Why is this motherfuck so goddamned important ta' Langley?"

"Because," said the Arab grudgingly, but in a matter of fact tone, "in his day, in his prime, he truly was the best covert man we had. That is the simple truth; it is no exaggeration, even as it pains me to say so."

"So what the hell happened ta' him? Ah mean, look at him. Ah've seen better lookin' beggars in Wuhan."

Djabouli looked up at the moon face of Richards and closed his briefcase with a sharp snap. "Apparently, not very much," he said coldly. "Goodbye Mr. Richards."

Chapter 15

Eli said nothing to his two escorts all the way the airport. He sat uncomfortably between Djabouli and Quentin, not his first choice of companionship for the flight to Hong Kong. Still, Eli was thrilled to finally leave the embassy after a very long week, even if the end of the journey did have the potential to ruin a lot more than just his day. After they were airborne, the little Arab handed Eli a sealed envelope with his name on the front and with the word, "CONFIDENTIAL" stamped in large red letters over it. "I was told to give you this and not to open it on pain of death," said Djabouli wryly. "I thought it best this time to follow instructions."

"That's a first," Eli said. He wondered what in the world Morgan could possibly say to him after all these years. How could he make up for what had happened with Jasper? How could he ever make up for the sellout in Nicaragua? The flood of memories brought back an equal flood of anger and Eli violently tore open the envelope and read the enclosed note to himself: "Rose, you SOB. I'm sendin' these two guys after ya' because I don't want ya' to damage any of my freshman agents. Please do me a favor and don't make their lives miserable by escapin.' I'd just have to scalp them bald-headed, and ya' don't want me to have to do somethin' nasty like that? I'm sure ya' remember what that was like. Anyway, I have an offer for ya' that I think you'll like. Morgan."

"How interesting," muttered Djabouli. "I can see from your expression that Mr. Morgan has made you a proposal. What kind of offer is this, I wonder?"

"I'm sure it's nothing you'd been interested in hearing about," Eli grimaced.

The somewhat bumpy flight arrived in Hong Kong on schedule and as the trio deplaned, Eli noticed a very familiar face amongst the teeming crowds of family and friends. Mai Lee's burly chauffeur, Baizhu, stared at them from a corner as they entered the terminal and nodded almost imperceptibly when he saw Eli had recognized him. Djabouli and the lumbering Quentin kept Eli more or less between them as they followed the "In Transit" signs towards the gate for their next flight. Just as they were about to enter the restricted area, a small group of heavily armed airport security guards approached the three men with their guns at the ready.

"Excuse me, gentlemen," said the young Chinese officer with a crisp delivery of the Queen's English. "May I see your passports, please?"

"What's all this, then?" demanded Djabouli,

fumbling in his coat pocket for his passport.

"Just a routine check, sir. Nothing to be alarmed about." The officer examined all three passports closely, glancing up at each of the men as he compared the pictures with reality. The young guy retained two of the passports, handing them to one of the guards, and returned Eli's illegal one with an apology. "Very sorry for the inconvenience, sir. Have a good day." Eli smiled and looked over at Djabouli, who was dumb-struck for a moment. "You two gentlemen will have to come with me," added the officer.

"What?" shouted the Arab. "What is this all about? Do you know who I am? I'll have you know I am on official business for the government of the United States of America and you have no right to detain me!"

The distinctive sound of several AR-15 machine gun bolts being locked back punctuated the young officer's request. "Very sorry sir, but you'll have to come just the same. You will have an opportunity to protest to your government, but first, if you please." His outstretched arm showed the way to the security office, and the guards gave Djabouli and Quentin each a brisk shove in the back with their guns to start the procession in motion.

"You'll hear about this," Djabouli shouted angrily as he was led away. "Rose, don't you go anywhere until we get back, or you will suffer greatly. Rose? Rose? I am warning you in the name of the United States, do not move!" The group shuffled off noisily down the crowded corridor.

"Say hello to Morgan when you see him," Eli

replied with a wave. "Tell him he can find me in Miami if he still wants to see me."

Baizhu walked over and motioned for Eli to follow him to the big Mercedes, which he'd blatantly parked in the space marked "SECURITY ONLY." They drove away from the airport quickly and were soon headed up towards the big house near the top of Victoria Peak. Eli was smugly satisfied with his good fortune and intended to thank Mai Lee appropriately at the first opportunity. Cheung's house was unusually quiet for a change, lacking the constant parade of advisors and managers that drifted through the place during Eli's previous visit. There was a palpable feeling of tension in the air as they pulled up to the massive wooden doors, and the old woman Eli expected was nowhere to be seen. In fact, Baizhu appeared to be the only employee in the place. Eli dismissed the odd impression with the thought that Cheung had perhaps given the staff the day off. He should have paid more attention to his innate sense of alarm.

Baizhu led Eli out onto the familiar terrace, where he fully expected to see Mai Lee beaming with joy at his return. When he glimpsed the guests on the terrace he tried to turn and run, but the stern-faced Baizhu applied a quick hammer lock to his right arm, pinning him to the cold floor. Before he could react, he felt the hard steel barrel of a 9 mm Beretta 92F shoved against the back of his head. That convinced him to stay.

"So, Mr. Rose, you return to us after all. How very happy I am to see you." Cheung smiled and extended his hand cordially, but quickly withdrew it with a laugh. "I was afraid I might never see you again. Oh, sorry. How rude of me. Perhaps you would like some tea first? Please, sit here next to my lovely niece."

Mai Lee sat rigidly at his side, her eyes downcast and red, a sure sign she'd been crying. The robotic chauffeur gave Eli a shove towards the table, and he lurched forwards and grabbed one of the white wrought iron chairs to steady himself.

"Please, Mr. Rose. I insist you sit here next to me. I want to congratulate you on your most brilliant foray and escape from the Mainland." The old man smiled and sipped his tea calmly, as though nothing out of the ordinary had occurred.

"I am so thrilled that you're pleased," Eli said sarcastically, rubbing his twisted shoulder. "This was one hell of a greeting, considering how *pleased* you are. Never mind the fact that you sold my ass to Old Tiger."

"Oh, come now my friend," he chuckled. "That was purely a business decision, and since you have returned to us after all, and rather miraculously I might add, I am bound to honor our original deal." He produced a large envelope from his coat pocket and slapped it crudely on the glass table top beside Eli. "I have included a $100,000 bonus on top of the agreed-upon fee for a job so excellently done."

Eli picked up the envelope and glanced at the contents to satisfy his curiosity. "So what was her part in all this?"

Mai Lee moved to speak but the old man raised his hand, a gesture clearly meant to stifle any response. "Well, you see that is the interesting part of this little adventure," he said slowly. "I have had the rather unfortunate displeasure of informing this charming young lady that she is not actually my niece."

The girl looked up at Eli with misty eyes, and it was immediately apparent that the old man wasn't joking. "You remember that interesting story I was telling you about her father and I, and our unlucky venture to the Mainland? Well, it was necessary for the good of the people to ensure the failure of that mission."

"For the good of the people?" Eli repeated slowly. "Crap, you're a double agent! How much did you get for turning her father in?"

"All you see around you," said the old man, opening his arms. "My position here in Hong Kong, and the financing to build all this. The Maoists were very pleased with my work, so they glorified me by allowing me to remain here permanently, provided I continued my counter-revolutionary activities."

"Charming. So I can count myself among the beneficiaries of your charade. I suppose I shouldn't feel like a complete fool."

"Not at all," he smiled broadly. "Actually, you were quite good, by far the most resourceful of all my guests. I consider it a great waste having to kill you."

"And the money?"

"Counterfeit, of course. When the police finally pull your body from the harbor, we will plant a story of your involvement with certain underworld elements, the same ones that aided your escape from custody today. That plus the money should silence any potential investigation into your visit."

"Well, you know that could be avoided." Eli started to feel his stomach tensing up into a knot, and he realized that the candle was burning very rapidly for him.

"Sorry," Cheung said with a short sigh, "but I could never trust you."

"Wait a minute," Eli shouted. "You can't do this without explaining a few things to me first."

"Well, perhaps I owe you at least that much. It might even be amusing to see your reactions to my answers. Please go ahead and ask me anything."

Eli's mind drew an instantaneous blank and he stammered, trying to regain his composure. "Tell me why...why someone was trying to kill us."

Cheung laughed and shook his head. "Well of course, that was the typical style of the Taipei government. I suspected they had been watching me for some time and I was hoping you would be resourceful enough to stay alive and continue the mission. And you exceeded my expectations!"

"And this deal you made with Old Tiger - why? I just don't get it."

The old man grinned in self satisfaction. "Of course Old Tiger's intelligence apparatus knew of your trip from the beginning and he indeed wanted to control you before your arrival in Haikou. However, I managed to salvage my interests by making that quaint little deal for you, and guaranteeing to him that you would be more of a help than a hindrance." Eli was about to ask another question when the old man continued on, unprompted. "The girl was of obvious use to us, but I have to congratulate myself on some wonderful long-range planning. When her father was disposed of, it was decided that she might someday be put to good use."

"Decided by whom, your people on the Mainland?" Eli interrupted.

"Yes. I was allowed to raise and educate her as I saw fit." Cheung stroked her long black hair with his thin hand but she pulled away in disgust. "Yes, my dear Mai Lee is as close to me as any daughter I would have ever had."

"So you duped her into believing she had to sell me out for the diamonds."

"Diamonds?" gasped the old man. "The diamonds were a partial reward for all these years of servitude to an ungrateful master. The new administration in Beijing has decided that I have outlived my usefulness here, and I must return to assume some obscure ministerial post. Can you imagine! Would you leave *this* for Beijing?" Eli nodded and smiled, trying to humor Cheung's ego while he frantically scanned the terrace in search of something to use as a weapon.

"No, my foolish friend," Cheung rambled. "All this trouble was not for a small handful of diamonds. *This* is what I wanted. *This* is what your precious Mai Lee was sent to retrieve." He pulled a tiny metal canister from his pocket and held it up for Eli to see. "And now you know the depth of her deceit." The old man was clearly enjoying himself.

"Microfilm," Eli sighed, finally enlightened after spending so much time in the dark. He felt terrible but at least he now understood the girl's motivation.

"Don't you think the plan was brilliant?" Cheung queried with keen interest, slapping his open hand on his knee. "This poor girl thought that I was working for the overthrow of the Communists, and that she was performing a loyal service for the future of her people. She never realized that by delivering the contents of the statue to me that she was also handing me a list of the names and addresses of all of the opposition leaders in China. With the diamonds in my left hand and the list to sell to the Communists in my right, *we* will have more money than you could ever imagine."

Mai Lee was sullen and depressed, dark with anger and sadness at having her world suddenly come crashing down around her. Eli was sad for her, but they both needed a way out, and he had to keep the old bastard occupied just a little longer. "I suppose I can guess the answer to my next question, but I'll ask anyway. Where did Old Tiger get off to?"

"Oh, yes," laughed Cheung. He waved at someone behind them and Eli just knew whose face would pop into view.

"My dear Mr. Rose, so good to see you again," grinned the drug lord, looking refined in his smartly tailored suit. "You know, you really made quite a mess of things for me. I had to allow you to escape even when I really wanted to kill you for exposing my operation. But you served *our* purpose well, nevertheless."

"Go on," Eli prayed. "This has been interesting. Why did you want me involved in the first place?"

Cheung and Old Tiger looked at one another, trying like spoiled children to decide which one would have the opportunity to tell Eli the secret. Old Tiger spoke up first and said, "Your presence covered a multitude of sins, Mr. Rose. The whole plan was a beautiful example of the principle of multiple working hypotheses. You see at first I saw you as a threat, but Mr. Cheung saw you as a tool to help recover his microfilm. Later, he convinced me that you could help us both by facilitating removal of the diamonds from Vietnam for me, and allowing Mai Lee to get them to him for sale here in Hong Kong. Your presence on the border only helped to legitimize the whole affair for the Chinese who, I might add, still believe you to have been in the employ of the CIA."

"So, honor amongst thieves. Will wonders never cease?" Eli shook his head, trying to distract them for a little while longer, searching desperately for some way out. "And the scar from the bullet in the neck?"

"Just an artful job of make-up," Cheung answered, smiling.

"And you really wanted me as part of the deal?" Eli said to Old Tiger.

"I never forget to settle an old score, Mr. Rose," he replied coldly. "I had fully intended to finish you until Mr. Cheung convinced me of your value. I still question whether that was a wise decision on my part considering the cost, but I can always move the operation to Myanmar."

"Yes, and it was such a shame for you to lose that pretty greenhouse of yours."

"Oh really?" Old Tiger chided. "You have heard something that I have not? I am sorry to disappoint you, my friend, but I was able to save more than one of my favorite little beauties."

"But the CIA told me........"

"Enough of this!" shouted Cheung impatiently. "I am now growing tired of your incessant questioning."

"I'm sorry," Eli interrupted, searching discretely over his shoulder for Baizhu. "I didn't want to offend you, but you did say that I could ask you anything."

"This is not a *James Bond* film Mr. Rose, and I will not answer every question before we kill you. We have had enough of your presence here. Now I will say good-bye, and I will pass on your regards to Mr. Amarón when I next see him. Once he is dealt with, there will be no chance that any of this will ever be discovered by the authorities."

Cheung waved at Baizhu and the burly chauffeur stepped up behind Eli and yanked him to his feet by his shirt collar. As he stood up, Eli heard the familiar click of Mai Lee's switchblade as it opened, and she slid it across the slick table top into his right hand. He grabbed it and swung his arm around behind his back, thrusting up when the blade struck home. Eli pivoted instantly and the chauffeur tumbled backwards onto the table, the blade jammed into his throat. Blood spurted from his carotid artery onto the table and the stone floor while Baizhu tried in vain to stem the flow with both hands. He dropped the Beretta to the ground as he reached for the gaping wound and it bounced just out of Eli's reach and landed behind a large potted palm.

Mai Lee sprang to her feet and pushed away from the flailing man, but Cheung caught her in a headlock from behind. Eli and Old Tiger were thinking the same thing because they collided as Eli dove for the unused pistol. Eli was stunned but managed to grab the black gun as it hit the hard floor. The old man fell on top of him and as if he was truly a tiger, choked Eli with one hand as he wrestled for the gun with the other. Eli shook off the fog of the collision and brought his left elbow up under Old Tiger's chin in a swift, crushing blow, and the old man sprawled backwards onto the stones. Eli rolled over intending to shoot Cheung, but instead saw him wrench Mai Lee by the neck, knocking her to her knees. Before he could squeeze the trigger, the old viper grabbed a handful of her beautiful jet black hair and smashed her head into the cold stone wall.

Eli froze when he saw her beautiful eyes roll up, and watched in disbelief as she fell sideways against the wall. He leveled the pistol at Cheung and pulled the trigger, but the shot flew wildly past him when Old Tiger kicked him in the ribs. Blood dripped from his shattered chin onto Eli's face as he stood over him, ready to smash his skull with a large pot. Eli again brought the Beretta up to fire, and this time landed one round from point blank range. The huge slug hit him in the forehead and sprayed his brains across the terrace. The dead man looked at Eli as if he was about to question what had just happened, but then collapsed on top of him in a heap. Eli rolled his corpse on to the stone floor and scrambled to his feet, looking for Cheung. He'd found Mai Lee's knife on the bloody table and held it to her throat, holding her limp head up by her hair.

"You won't kill me and risk the girl's life," he stammered. "Drop the gun or I will kill her."
"Go ahead!" Eli shouted. "She's already dead."
Cheung glanced down quizzically at her limp figure for a split second, just long enough for Eli to raise and fire the 9 mm. The bullet struck him high on the right shoulder and spun him backwards against the wall like a rag doll. The knife flew over the barrier and probably landed half way down the mountain side. Mai Lee slid back against the wall, comatose. Eli walked closer to the old buzzard with the gun pointed rigidly at his head and said, "Now, Mr. Cheung, I will take the microfilm."
The pain in his eyes mixed with fear as he tried, with trembling hands, to retrieve the small metal canister. He dropped it onto the blood-soaked table and stood, bent at the waist, looking ashen and beaten. "Mr. Rose," he croaked in a raspy voice, "you are a fair-minded man. You won't kill me in cold blood."
Eli looked down at Mai Lee's prostrate form and his anger boiled over like a waterfall. "My good friend, Mr. Cheung............I believe you dropped your knife."

Epilogue

"Rita!" Eli yelled, running through the door out of breath. "Any messages?"

"Yes, Eli, you have a couple. They're on your desk with the mail."

Eli hated mornings and Rita knew it. Being on time was never one of his strong suits. Too many years in Costa Rica had sapped any desire for punctuality, and the frenetic pace of Miami was so hard to get accustomed to after sleepy old Playa Coco. It took him awhile, but Eli was finally able to find a familiar face that understood just what a pain the adjustment was for him.

Rita was perfect; there was his cup of triple strength Cuban coffee, resting comfortably next to the sports section of the *Miami Herald*. She knew there was no other way to jump-start his brain at such an early hour, so Eli allowed her great liberties with her attitude. He propped his feet up on the desk and slowly sifted through the junk and old bills. He glanced at the paper. "Hey," he shouted. "Looks like the 'Canes might have a pretty good team this year."

"Ah ha," droned Rita from the other room.
"Yeah, they've got this kid named Toretta. Seems really talented. Maybe he'll amount to something." Eli never understood how anyone could function before nine in the morning, and he tossed the mail aside and concentrated on the sports page. "So.........Hey, are you still out there?"
"Yeah, I'm here. What do ya' want now?" Rita groused.
"No calls for an hour, Ok? I've got to get my head on straight first."
"Yeah, Ok," she said indifferently.

At least Eli knew that she'd do what he asked, no matter how sour she made it sound. But even Rita was sympathetic at times, at least as much as she could be since his return to Miami. Eli's re-adjustment had not gone as well as he'd hoped, and he felt fortunate to have been able to locate her again after so many years. Rita had started working for the DEA as a file clerk after Eli relocated to the tropics. She'd progressed up the government ladder in a short time, all the way to office manager when he called her out of the blue. The poor girl nearly died when she realized it was him, and it took her about three seconds to agree to come back to work as his chief logistics officer/secretary. So as transitions go, things could have been worse. The handful of diamonds Eli recovered from the late Mr. Cheung netted him enough money to finance the new office of Brickell Avenue Associates for another five years. After that, he'd probably lose interest and move back to Costa Rica anyway.

The two messages were both from Jim Morgan in Langley, probably about another "service contract." Eli hated like hell to do that kind of work for Morgan but it kept the cash flowing in, and in the "lost and found" business, cash flow is everything. Every time he thought about how Morgan had abandoned him after China, his blood pressure went through the roof. At least he never got the microfilm. But because of everything that had happened, especially that thing at Kai Tak with Ahmed and Quentin, the only way Eli could keep the Brickell Avenue address was to cut the same kind of on-demand deal with him that he'd had to arrange after the first Costa Rican fiasco. There he was, right back in the same place he was when he took off to meet poor Eva Lawrence that first time almost 20 years ago. Eli still felt a twinge when he thought of the girl. Such a terrible waste!

Most of the mail was not worth reading, with the exception of one plain envelope postmarked in Hong Kong. Eli could smell her perfume through the thin outer cover before he'd even opened it. The letter slid out smoothly, along with a small photograph.

"Dear Eli, I do miss you terribly and wish you all my love. Things are going well here now that the courts have finally decided that I should be the legal heir to all of Uncle's assets. The inquest did indeed rule his death a homicide, most likely due to the falling out he had with Old Tiger. They say Old Tiger was the one who injured me, and that when Uncle came to my aid, Old Tiger shot him and he fell. If it hadn't been for your quick action shooting Old Tiger, I'm certain he would have finished me as well."

"I still have no memory of that last day, and the doctors say I may never remember what happened. But with physical therapy I am regaining my strength at a more rapid pace every day, and soon I expect to have full use of my arm again. I think of you often and look forward to the day when we can be together again. The feeling of your last kiss will stay on my lips forever. I love you, Mai Lee. PS - When I am well I will finally take that trip to Rio we spoke about. I do hope you can come. I will contact you with all the details soon. For me, you will always be the last and the best. Love, Mai Lee."

Eli crumpled the letter tightly and threw it into his basketball trash can. The note landed cleanly on the bottom with a hollow thud, and he muttered, "Two points. The crowd goes crazy. Give that man a Miller." The picture revealed the same, sweet girl Eli had left at the hospital in Hong Kong, though her hair was much shorter now. She looked great and thankfully had not regained her memory of what really happened that day on the terrace. Eli told her the whole story when he'd visited her in the hospital, but it was the story he'd concocted for the police. At least she could keep her illusions and live with herself, not knowing how her "Uncle" had really misled and used her most of her life. It was better that way, but Eli felt terrible. What was he doing? He should be there with her, not in Miami! Eli tossed the picture onto his desk next to the familiar black Beretta that was now as close to him as any member of the family.

The intercom on his desk buzzed annoyingly and snapped him back to reality. "What is it?" Eli demanded angrily, looking at his watch. "Rita, I thought I told you one hour. What's the matter, can't you tell time?"

"You told me no calls, damn it. This ain't a call. I bet you'll never guess what the cat dragged in this time. Someone who says he's known you for a long time. Want me to call the cops?"

Eli sighed. "No, send the guy in, and stop cursing!" The hot-tempered little *Cubana* was the only person Eli ever let speak to him like that. He remembered the first time she interviewed for the job 10 years ago, flaunting her tight little ass in his face with impunity. She had the kind of brass Eli liked and he considered her a rare and true friend because of her honesty.

The office door swung open a crack and it was suddenly old home week. A face Eli thought had long since faded into the fog of his past smiled at him once more. "So, Vicente," Eli said without emotion, "how have you been?"

"Ok, Eli. Ok." He grinned broadly, and his accent

was just as flavorful as ever.

Eli looked at him standing there in his *guayabera* shirt and khaki pants and was seared by *déjà vu*. "You don't look too bad old man, considering it's been almost six years. A little thicker around the middle and maybe a little less hair, but not too bad. Have a seat"

He sat across the desk with perfect posture, the way Eli always remembered, and pulled a cigarette from his dented silver case. "Do you mind if I......?"

"No, go ahead. It'll just kill you quicker."

Vicente puffed deeply on the cigarette and brought it to life. With a wave of his now cigarette-bound hand he added, "And this is what you want for me?"

"Hell, I don't know," Eli said, staring down at the Beretta. "After what you did setting me up with Cheung I should shoot you in your Cuban ass right where you sit." He sighed and rubbed a hand across his thinning hair. "But I guess I want to know what's on your mind first. So what's up, Vicente? Why are you here?"

"Is just a social call, my boy," he smiled, pushing the cigarette into the heel of his shoe.

"Come on, cut the crap and get to the point. What the hell are you doing here?"

"Eli, I come to see you for to ask you for my old job." He calmly tossed the burnt stub into the trash can.

"Your old job! Good Lord what nerve! Hey Rita," Eli shouted. "Get in here for a minute. You may need to translate something for me." She wiggled her way into the office with her steno pad and sat down opposite Vicente, flashing him a toothy smile "He says he wants his old job back," Eli said to her, reflecting his anger.

"He sells me out to the Chinese and still has the balls to come in here and ask for his old job. Translate this into Cuban for me so I know he gets it. Ask him, is this some kind of goddamn joke or something?"

Rita looked at Eli like he was kidding, so he shouted, "What do I have to do, spell it out for ya'?"

She looked at Vicente indifferently and said in perfect English, "Eli wants to know, is this some kind of goddamn joke or something?"

Eli slapped his forehead with anger. Vicente just sat there calmly, completely unflustered but intent on pursuing his request.

"I want my old job, Eli. And you should want me with you here. We were a great team in the old days."

"That was six years ago," Eli grunted. "Another lifetime. You remember that crap you pulled in Nicaragua with Morgan, don't you? Well, you almost got me killed." He stared out the window at the cars ten stories below. "Why don't you take a flying jump out the window? It would save me some trouble."

"Eli, what happen in Nicaragua was no my fault. You know Morgan set you up to get Jasper. He fool me also. Think about it. You know it make sense."

"Not a good enough answer, old man. Why do you *really* want to do this? What's in it for you, besides the money? And what do I get out of it, except a tired-ass old *gusano* I can't trust?"

The gray fox walked over to Eli and put his arm on Eli's shoulder. "You are my only family, Eli. Without you these past years, I have been a lost soul in this world. We need each other; men like us never have anyone else. We are a team and more than that. You know it true."

"Yeah, yeah," echoed Rita as she shoved a stick of chewing gum into her mouth. "Listen to him, Eli. We can have the team together again, just like the old days."

Eli glared at her and she abruptly shut up. "Pretty flimsy reason," he said. Eli rose slowly and began pacing his office from one side to the other, staring out his window and back again at his two companions. Maybe...........I don't know."

"My boy, we cover all the old ground six year ago. You know it was an accident there in the jungle, with Jasper and the girl. I look for you, you know this." Vicente waved his hands in the air as if God himself would enter the discussion on his side. "I am thinking this is still the problem, *si*? Not that snake Cheung. I think you need the work so I give him your name. That is all and no more."

"So you were only looking out for me this whole time. Do I have that right?"

"*Si* my boy, that is the truth." Vicente turned in his chair to look at Eli.

Rita stared at the two men, not sure what to expect. Anger, reconciliation, sadness? "Look Boss," she said in a half whisper, "I think he means it. Eli, you can't do everything alone. Ya' gotta' have someone in your life."

When Rita spoke in anything but a growl or a yell it conveyed sincerity, and that wasn't lost on Eli. He stared out the window and for the first time in a long time looked beyond the shallowness of what he felt at the moment. "So what if you're right. How do we get back to where we were, maybe where we should have been from the beginning? It's been a very long time."

"Many year, that much is true." Vicente rose and approached Eli, both arms extended. "But we have both learn so much. We no are the same people like before." He embraced his former protégé firmly and whispered, "Now is only you and me. No more games, no more lies. Only you and me." He hugged Eli again and then held him at arm's length.

Eli felt sad and he knew why. He'd kept Vicente at a distance since that night in Managua when he was sold out to the Sandinistas. He could have contacted him but he didn't know who to trust after that, so he just cut everyone off and drowned his sorrows in a bottle of Costa Rican rum. The relationship had been a dry shell of what it was before, a sham and nothing more. Eli had no one and that loneliness was not a feeling he dealt with well or often. He'd excluded the only person left from his past that truly cared about him and that hurt. He didn't like that feeling and avoided it like the plague, but here it was again. Eli knew he had a clear choice presented to him now, and he could either let his pride and misplaced anger dictate his future or he could take Vicente's words at face value and trust him. Eli grabbed his old mentor and hugged him back.

"Just because you've caught me in a moment of weakness don't think this means you get a full partnership again."

Rita smiled broadly and clapped her hands while Vicente patted Eli's back. "No worry about this. You are the boss. I do what you say."

Eli sat back down and smiled for the first time in a long time. He felt.............happy.

"So Eli, now I tell you something you must hear but maybe you don't like."

Eli rolled his eyes and sighed audibly. Rita stopped her gum in mid chew. The ex-protégé opened his palms and said, "Ok, what is it now?"

"Forget about the girl, my boy. It no work in this business."

Eli stared at him silently for a few seconds, trying to stifle his emotions. Maybe he was just vulnerable or once again Vicente could be right. Rita stared at him, expecting the worst.

But Eli was in the right mood, especially after their reconciliation. He thought about the situation as honestly and objectively as he'd ever done. *The idea is easier to swallow coming from Vicente*, Eli thought. And he knew it was true. He knew he'd never see Mai Lee again, that it would never have worked out with her anyway. They were living completely different lives that just happened to cross for a few weeks last year. Any spark he felt had faded. Did he miss what they shared or what he *thought* they shared?

The way Vicente put it seemed so final, so cut and dried, so simple. But in the end there is beauty in simplicity, and Eli could see that the simple solution was likely the best one as well. "*Si, amigo,*" Eli sighed, resigned to the inevitability of the decision. Any notion that he might have had to toss his new life in the can and jump a plane for Hong Kong lay in the trash with that crumpled letter.

Vicente smiled affectionately, Rita clapped again excitedly, and Eli couldn't stay angry with either of them. He knew Vicente was right all along, that they were two of a kind, for better or for worse. There was just no point arguing about it. "Listen. One more thing – don't drop my name to anyone else without telling me about it first, Ok?"

"I promise," the old man grinned.

"So old friend, even though we are not full partners…."

"Yet," inserted Vicente.

"Even though we are not full partners *yet*," said Eli, "I think we need to change the sign on the door. You never know – it will probably help draw some business from Eighth Street."

"This is crazy," said Vicente proudly. "This is you office, no is mine. You are the boss."

The three of them began a vigorous discussion about whose name should go where and how to change the stationary when a stylishly dressed young girl interrupted with a knock on Eli's door. "Excuse me. I'm sorry to interrupt but I'm looking for Mr. Eli Rose."

"You found him," Eli said, standing to greet her. Vicente leaped from his chair and bowed, offering her the seat. She smiled and sat down with Vicente standing stiffly beside her, inspecting her clothes. He gave Eli a wink, as if to say that they would probably make a lot money on this job, for a change.

"So, Miss............."

"McHenry. Josephine McHenry. You can call me Jo."

"So, Miss McHenry, how can we help you?" Eli smiled expectantly but without emotion.

"Well," she hesitated, looking askance at Rita and Vicente. Rita hopped up from her chair and excused herself, closing the door behind her. "Well," she repeated, "I need some help finding two people."

"I don't wish to be impolite, by why don't you go to the police? They deal with this sort of thing all the time. They're really pretty good at it," Eli said, trying not to be impatient with her. *It's a game*, he thought. *No truth here. What does she really want?*

"They suggested I talk to you. They said you were the best man for this kind of job."

"Ok great. I'll have to thank the Assistant Chief next time I see him for that glowing endorsement. So what kind of job is this that only I can do?" Eli was running out of patience.

"It's my mother and father. They took our boat out to the Bahamas three weeks ago and haven't returned. I can't find out anything and the police won't help because they say it's out of their jurisdiction. The Bahamian authorities say that there's no evidence of any crime and that Mom and Dad probably just wanted to get away from the rat race. But I think something *bad* has happened to them."

"I don't know, Miss McHenry," Eli sighed.

"Jo."

"Fine, Jo. This really isn't the type of work we do but I can assign my best man here, Vicente Amarón, to do some preliminary work on your case. Why don't you two discuss this in the conference room where you can have some privacy?"

Jo pouted and frowned like a scolded child. "I was told *you* were the best man, Mr. Rose."

"Sorry," Eli smiled, enjoying the opportunity to dump her off on Vicente, "but *he's* the best man we've got."

Vicente shook his head vigorously and smiled, returning the favor to Eli just like old times. "No is true, *señorita.* I am sorry but Sr. Eli is the best. I am only the next best man."

www.ingramcontent.com/pod-product-compliance
Lightning Source LLC
Chambersburg PA
CBHW060800120626
46557CB00001B/44